Professional father of one—requires help with s̶o̶m̶e̶ irregular babysitting d̶u̶t̶i̶e̶s̶ i̶n̶ ̶r̶e̶turn for reduced a̶c̶c̶o̶m̶o̶d̶a̶t̶i̶o̶n̶.

Rural p̶r̶o̶p̶e̶r̶t̶y̶ ̶w̶i̶t̶h̶ acreage—animals t̶o̶ ̶c̶a̶r̶e̶ ̶f̶o̶r̶.

Need to be flexible.

Experience with children essential.

There *had* to be a catch, Charlotte had decided as she had driven her ancient car up the driveway of Adam's farm for her interview and glimpsed the gorgeous sprawling property. But, most importantly of all, she'd promptly melted as she'd entered the kitchen—a massive family room set behind it, and on the sofa in the middle a delicious two-year-old who had happily climbed all over her the second she had sat down.

And there was the catch—the gorgeous Hamish Adams.

BACHELOR DADS
Single Doctor… Single Father!

At work they are skilled medical professionals, but at home, as soon as they walk in the door, these eligible bachelors are on full-time fatherhood duty!

These devoted dads still find room in their lives for love…

It takes very special women to win the hearts of these dedicated doctors, and a very special kind of caring to make these single fathers full-time husbands!

THE SINGLE DAD'S MARRIAGE WISH

BY
CAROL MARINELLI

MILLS & BOON™
Pure reading pleasure

All the characters in this book have no existence outside the imagination of the author, and have no relation whatsoever to anyone bearing the same name or names. They are not even distantly inspired by any individual known or unknown to the author, and all the incidents are pure invention.

First published in Great Britain 2007
Harlequin Mills & Boon Limited,
Eton House, 18-24 Paradise Road, Richmond, Surrey TW9 1SR

© Carol Marinelli 2007

ISBN-13: 978 0 263 85260 8

Set in Times Roman 10½ on 12¾ pt
03-0907-44006

Printed and bound in Spain
by Litografia Rosés, S.A., Barcelona

Carol Marinelli recently filled in a form where she was asked for her job title, and was thrilled, after all these years, to be able to put down her answer as writer. Then it asked what Carol did for relaxation, and, after chewing her pen for a moment, she put down the truth—writing. The third question asked: What are your hobbies? Well, not wanting to look obsessed or, worse still, boring, she crossed the fingers on her free hand and answered swimming and tennis. But, given that the chlorine in the pool does terrible things to her highlights, and the closest she's got to a tennis racket in the last couple of years is watching the Australian Open—I'm sure you can guess the real answer!

Dear Reader

Phew—I don't tend to write from my male character's point of view. But for this story I made an exception.

My heroine in this book, Charlotte Porter, is an amazing woman who spun into my imagination—and, rather than try to fathom her out and then try to translate her, I decided it might be better to let my hero Hamish (okay—he's not *my* hero, he's Charlotte's) work to get to know her alongside the reader.

I confess to a few giggles as I wrote—perhaps because I knew what was happening—and more than a few tears for the very same reason.

I hope you love the story as much as I did.

Happy reading

Carol Marinelli

CHAPTER ONE

'HELLO beautiful!'

Breezing into the examination cubicle, Charlotte's wide smile never moved an inch as two scowling faces turned around at the sound of her cheerful voice.

A child who wasn't particularly beautiful.

And a man who most definitely was.

'I wasn't talking about him!' Charlotte's dark curls danced in their ponytail as she gestured towards the doctor in the corner, watching, as the pinched little face of her patient delivered one of his very rare smiles. A smile so bright, so wide, that it ought to be utilised more.

'I'm Charlotte, by the way,' she added to the other scowling face, as she checked little Andy's IV site and recorded his hourly observations. 'Charlotte Porter.'

'Hamish,' he responded, barely looking up as he wrote out an X-ray request. 'Hamish Adams.'

So *this* was the famous Hamish, Charlotte thought, sneaking a surreptitious glance at his name tag and then at the man himself.

Hamish Adams—Emergency Consultant.

Since she'd started here in Emergency two weeks ago, his name had cropped up a million and one times.

"Hamish likes it done this way."

"Hamish insists on that."

Hamish, Hamish Hamish…

And here was the man himself—and *very* nice he was, too. Tall but not too tall, Charlotte decided, trying not to get caught peeking! Slightly damp, jet hair flopped over his forehead as he resumed writing, and those hazel eyes that had briefly looked over as she'd walked into the cubicle had had her heart rate accelerating a touch. Dressed in theatre blues topped with a rather shabby white coat, he'd clearly not long rolled out of bed. His scowling face was unshaven and he smothered a yawn as he filled out some X-ray and blood request forms. Still, even if he hadn't had time for shave, he'd clearly hit the shower this morning, and it wasn't just his damp hair that gave him away—he had that nice *clean man* smell about him, which added just a touch of pink to Charlotte's cheeks when he next spoke. 'I want Andy to have erect and supine abdo X-rays and then some more bloodwork.' Hamish peered at his watch. 'It isn't urgent, though—I'll draw the blood now and get it off, but he can wait another hour or so till X-Ray opens at nine. If you go round with him, can you ask the radiographer to pull his old films—?'

'I'm going off duty in a moment,' Charlotte responded, taking the slips, 'but I'll certainly pass your orders on for you. Right, Andy, I just popped in to say goodbye—I'll check the admission book when I come in later in the week and see where you ended up.'

'Will you come and see me on the ward if I'm still here in the hospital?'

'Absolutely.' Charlotte grinned but it faded a touch as she saw Hamish's frown, wondering what she must have said to offend him. Emergency nurses often popped up to the wards to catch up on patients—it was the only continuity offered to them. Andy had presented in the newly named Northern District Emergency Department at 4:00 a.m. after a night of crying with abdominal pain. What made his presentation a concern, though, was that it was his third in the last two months and, having read his notes and spoken at length with his exhausted mother and Andy himself, there was a big unvoiced question as to whether Andy was actually ill or struggling from the effects of severe teasing at school.

If a touch of extra attention helped, then Charlotte was more than happy to give it—whatever Hamish Adams thought!

It wasn't Charlotte's offer to catch up with her patient that had Hamish frowning, though—it was confusion. He could have sworn she'd just come *on* duty rather than going off! She was just so bright, and fresh, *so* unlike most people at the end of an eleven-hour shift.

So unlike most people, Hamish was about to find out.

'Where on earth did you get these?' She stared in mock horror at the X-ray and blood request forms he had given her. 'Don't you know these are banned!'

'What?'

'These forms, they say Camberfield General—didn't anyone think to tell you about the name change?'

He gave a dry smile at her sarcasm. Since its inception Hamish felt as if he'd been sitting in meetings for ever—it was almost *all* anyone senior *had* spoken about. Camberfield sat a couple of hours from the city of Melbourne—a delightful semi-rural town that had all the benefits of being close enough to be able to get to the city but still untouched enough to completely escape it. The hospital had served both the local and wider community well, but in a bureaucratic attempt to *streamline* services and *improve* patients' access to facilities, someone, somewhere, at some point in time had come up with the *brilliant* idea of closing down a few scattered cottage hospitals and upgrading Camberfield General—so that they were now a major trauma centre, covering such a vast area that Hamish had, in one of the meetings, made the rather surly suggestion that the patients be offered a rewards programme for all the hours they'd spend stuck in planes or helicopters just to get to hospital!

'I'm sure the radiographer and haematologist won't mi—'

'Oh, but they will!' Charlotte interrupted, and put on a very formal voice as she quoted the latest memo that had been handed out. 'Staff are again reminded that *no* procedures will be undertaken unless the correct patient requests forms are filled in. So,' she said, reverting to her more usual, cheery voice, 'you'd better write them all out again. But first you'd better empty out your pockets.'

'I'll throw them out later.'

'You won't.' Charlotte shook her head. 'You'll mean to, of course, but the next thing you know you'll have your poor patient being wheeled out of X-Ray minus a film. We've all been caught out with that one—and, anyway, they're *not* to be thrown out. We've been told they're to be cut into little squares and made into scrap paper…' He blinked as she snapped her fingers. 'Come on—hand it all over!'

He was about to tell this nurse *exactly* where to take her strange humour, but as the little boy he had barely managed to extricate two words from during his examination started to actually giggle, even Hamish managed a smile as he played along and handed over the pads.

'All of it!' Charlotte warned. And, like a teenager caught smoking, he dug into his white coat pockets and handed over all the paraphernalia that filled them—CT request slips, MRI imaging… Pad after pad came out. In fact, the only reason Hamish still wore a white coat was because the pockets were incredibly deep. 'I know it's hard to let go, but you'll thank me for this in the end.'

'Show the doctor the face!' Andy giggled, a different boy from the one Hamish had just examined.

'*That*,' Charlotte said firmly, 'was for your eyes only!' He watched in surprise as this confident woman actually blushed and suddenly busied herself tucking the blanket tighter around her patient.

'Show him!' Andy begged, then looked over at Hamish. 'Charlotte was picked on when she was my age!' This most reticent patient was opening up like a flower in the sun now that Charlotte was in the cubicle. Realising that more could be achieved in the next couple of minutes than any examination he might order, Hamish actually clicked off his pen and hung the notes at the end of the trolley, raising an eyebrow at the mysterious Charlotte and not believing it for a second. Nothing in her confident, outgoing demeanour indicated a damaged childhood—*and*, Hamish rather reluctantly noted, there was nothing in her striking looks that would make her a target for the hell inflicted by school bullies. Her long, dark mass of curls had, at some point, been scooped up into a ponytail, but nothing was going to contain them. Chocolate-brown ringlets were popping out everywhere, and her cornflower-blue eyes were as vivid and bright as her smile.

Surely she'd have been the most popular girl in the school, Hamish thought, only Charlotte was sticking to her story.

'Really?'

'Really!' Charlotte nodded. 'Mercilessly, actually. I lived for the bell at three-thirty so I could go home— well, four o'clock actually.'

'Did they tease you while you waited for your mum?'

'I got the school bus.' Charlotte gave a dramatic sigh. 'Unfortunately so did the rest of them.'

'They called her Hop-Along,' Andy explained to an intrigued Hamish.

'Did they, now?' He still didn't believe her for a second, but was delighted to see his patient teetering on the edge of revealing a painful part of himself. 'Well, that can't have been very nice. Do the kids call you names at school, too, Andy?'

'All the time.' Andy gave a small shrug but it was loaded with pain, his voice fading, hands pleating the sheet as he stared down at them.

'Sucks, doesn't it?' Charlotte offered—which probably wouldn't have been his choice of words, but they clearly summed up how Andy felt because finally he nodded, a fat tear rolling down his cheek as for the first time he admitted to a grown-up what had been happening.

'They all hate me.'

'Because they don't know you,' Charlotte said gently as Hamish watched on—a tiny tickle at the back of his throat as he watched this little guy who had been through so much in his short life being gently guided by this incredibly perceptive nurse. And whether she was telling the truth or not, it really didn't matter—she was everything this little boy needed right now. 'All they see is the glasses and your poor skin...' She reached out and stroked his arm, raw red and silver with one the of the worst cases of psoriasis he'd ever seen in a child—and adult too, come to that—but her touch wasn't just about compassion, it was showing the little boy, as his peers didn't, that he wasn't infectious or *dirty*, giving him the necessary human contact he so frequently missed out on.

'They say I'm thick—that I was born dumb.'

'They're the stupid ones, then,' Charlotte said firmly. 'They're the ones who don't know what they're talking about. Lots of famous people have dyslexia—though off the top of my head I can't think of one.'

'Da Vinci!' Hamish offered.

'Who?' Andy frowned.

'Don't worry, honey.' She shot a thanks but, no, thanks glance at Hamish. I'll find out some names of people with dyslexia that you actually know, but there are lots and I promise that if you keep trying, one day you'll work out how to deal with all of this…' Thick, hot tears were coursing down his cheeks now and she scooped him into a hug. 'You truly will! I never thought I'd get rid of my eye patch,' she said. 'I thought I'd have it for ever and ever—but things change, they really do. And when you're happier in yourself, let me tell you, *everything* changes—even your skin will start to improve…'

'You reckon?' Andy sniffed.

'I'm positive, but even if it doesn't, you'll be too busying having fun to notice! But first you've got to get happy here…' She touched his little chest and Hamish made no move to speak—nothing he could say now could make a dent in what Charlotte was saying.

'Is it really that easy?'

'Oh, it's not easy to be happy.' Charlotte shook her head and smiled down at him. 'It takes a lot of work—but the more you practice, the easier it gets.'

'They tease me all the time!' Andy looked over at Hamish. 'Just like they teased Charlotte—they called her Dumbo as well because one of her ears stuck out…and her teeth!' he added. 'Please, Charlotte, show him the face.'

Despite Hamish's rather astonishing good looks—despite the fact she'd heard something from the other staff about him being single, or rather widowed—wowing him with first impressions and a quick flirt had never been Charlotte's intention when she'd stepped in the cubicle—but to have the opportunity so cruelly obliterated, to be begged to show herself to this rather fabulous man in such a tragic light wasn't an opportunity she was keen to grab and run with. But looking at Andy's eager face, seeing him blink expectantly behind his thick glasses, his little hand scratching a large angry patch on his arm, Charlotte swallowed her mortification. With a groan of submission, she popped her hand behind her left ear in a practised move till it was waving like the said Dumbo, stuck out her top teeth and let her left eye roll inwards, just as she had a few hours earlier, but, Hamish noted, instead of collapsing back on the pillow in peals of laughter, as most eight-year-olds would, Andy turned a rather eager face to his doctor.

'See!' he exclaimed. 'Charlotte was *really* ugly and she's beautiful now, isn't she?' Not quite so unlike most eight-year-olds, Hamish noted dryly to himself—young Andy was more than capable of very direct and rather inappropriate observations. 'Isn't she beautiful?' Andy demanded.

'Er, yes…' Hamish nodded, giving a small cough. 'Charlotte, might I have a quick word outside before you go off duty? Andy…' As Charlotte gratefully ducked out of the cubicle he gave her a few seconds' grace to fan her flaming cheeks as he spoke to his patient. 'I'll be back in to speak to you shortly.'

He joined Charlotte. 'Thanks for that.' He didn't really look at her as he spoke. 'I know you should have finished your shift ages ago.'

'I don't mind—it's just good that he's talking.'

'It's a start.' Hamish nodded. 'I've seen Andy on his last couple of admissions with abdominal pain but have barely been able to get two words out of him. I strongly suspected, though, that bullying might be if not all of his problem then at least a significant part of it. Did you speak to his mother?'

'For a little while,' Charlotte said. 'She's breastfeeding a new baby so she's had to pop home. She said that he's always struggled to fit and been teased, but in the last few weeks he's been coming home with dirty clothes, his glasses were broken last week, that's why he's wearing those awful things, though Andy insists he fell over…' She gave a small shake of her head at the improbability. 'I think the teasing might be turning physical…'

'Bastards!' Hamish responded, and maybe it was a touch inappropriate, but this was emergency and, the world over, emergency staff didn't hold back on speaking their minds—it was the only thing that kept them sane. But, instead of agreeing with him as most emergency nurses would have, instead of adding a caustic comment of her own, he was more than a touch taken back when Charlotte let out a small smile.

'Oh, they're everywhere!' As blue as her eyes were, as pretty as the mouth was that smiled back at him, she delivered a surprisingly scathing yet very astute response. 'Young Andy's just going to have to learn how to deal with them if he wants to get on in life!'

'He's eight!' Hamish said abruptly.

'Then he's not too old to learn a few new tricks! Do you think there's anything going on with his abdomen?'

'All his tests to date have been normal, but I don't want to dismiss it,' Hamish said wisely. 'It would be all too easy to put it down to social problems but there could well be something going on so I'm going to speak to the surgeons and get him admitted. He could well have irritable bowel syndrome from stress alone. Still…' Hamish scratched a very nice jaw. 'He certainly needs admitting for his psoriasis—that has to be brought under control. Kenneth Miller, the hospital's dermatologist, is quite a leader in psoriasis. I'm surprised Andy hasn't already been referred to him, considering that's the worst case I've seen.'

'According to his mum, it's really flared up in the last few weeks. She's taken him to the doctor and he's changed his medication…he's having all his topical treatments.'

'Well, it's clearly not working. I'm going to get Kenneth to come and take a look—'

'And if he could talk to someone, a child psychologist perhaps,' Charlotte broke in, quietly delighted that this emergency consultant was thinking along the same lines as her—addressing not just the presenting problem but the bigger picture.

'To help him learn some new tricks?' Hamish asked with a distinctly dry note—but his sarcasm didn't touch her.

'Let's hope so! His mum's saving up for some more fashionable glasses—I know it's not going to make a massive difference, but if he could just get a shred of confidence…'

'Well, he certainly needs some. Though I admit that I saw a different side to him when he opened up in there, I'm sure he's depressed—and certainly he's suffering from anxiety.'

'You know…' she chewed her lip thoughtfully '…just one friend would make such a difference to that little guy. One friend to play with, one party to be invited to…'

'One magic wand!' Hamish gave a rueful smile. 'Can you write down your findings for me?'

'Done.' Charlotte smiled. 'Well, nearly—I've just got a few lines to add before I head off.'

'Thanks.'

More than a few lines, it would seem—she was still there at the nurses' station, just finishing off, when he came back from a prolonged conversation with young Andy.

'Here…' She handed him a page of neatly written notes. 'I went into a bit more detail, given how much he spoke to me.'

'Thanks for that.' Hamish nodded appreciatively, glancing down at her words—his sales pitch to various specialties suddenly made easier by her diligently recorded notes. 'Well, 'night, Charlotte. Have a nice sleep.' It was a casual goodbye often made as night staff went off duty, one you normally called out without even looking up, so why didn't it feel so casual, why, instead of sitting down and writing up his own notes, why, instead of getting on with his *day*, was he listening as Charlotte spoke about hers?

'Chance of sleeping would be a fine thing! I've got an interview at nine.'

'An interview—oh, was this just a casual shift, then?'

'No…' She was pulling off her stethoscope and hair tie and placing them in the largest handbag Hamish had ever seen, running her hands through her hair. He watched as a mass of dark curls fluffed into a cloud, then, without even attempting to hide what she was doing, boldly she whipped out a mirror, sat on a stool in the middle of the nurse's station and preened herself, adding a dash of mascara followed by a quick coat of lip gloss, chatting all the time. 'I'm permanent in Emergency—well, as long as I survive my three-month probation period! I started here couple of weeks ago.'

'So why the interview?' Hamish asked—and with good reason. The last thing he needed on his team was exhausted nurses juggling two jobs. Not that she looked exhausted, she literally oozed energy and vitality. Now she was popping her make-up back into her bag, yet still she rummaged through it, producing a bottle and adding a squirt of perfume to her neck and wrists, enveloping them both in a cloud of the scent that had first hit him when she'd entered Andy's cubicle.

'Charlotte!' Helen, the charge nurse, scolded as she walked into the work station, her fabulous Dublin accent which had survived unscathed for more than forty years in Australia ringing out for all to hear. 'You can't be spraying perfume here—people have allergies.'

'To a tinsy bit of perfume?' Charlotte laughed, and

to Hamish's surprise Helen smiled—Helen, who normally looked as if she'd sucked on a lemon for breakfast, was actually cracking a smile as Charlotte actually answered her back. 'Surely it's way better than that awful antiseptic spray.'

'This is a hospital, not a boudoir! Ooh, look at you, sitting there, putting on make-up and glamming yourself up right where the patients can see—I'm getting too old for all this.'

'Rubbish.' Charlotte gave a cheeky wink. 'You know what they say—you're only as old as the man you feel!'

'Take it outside, Charlotte,' Helen attempted to scold, but to Hamish's stunned amazement she wasn't just blushing but laughing as well. 'You're shocking!'

'I'm out of here.' Charlotte grinned, jumping off the stool and leaving Hamish with his question unanswered.

'She's a good girl really,' Helen said, picking up a can of antiseptic spray and attempting to douse the area, tutting when she realised it was empty. 'As dizzy as a spinning top and talks non-stop, mind you, but she's a good worker—got a good few years of experience in the country behind her. They breed good nurses out there. The pan room's never been cleaner and she's put away all the linen. And she's just so much fun. Did you see the notice she put up on the staff board? You should take a look! And patients love her too, she can charm anyone. I'll go and get another can of freshener. Would you like a drink, Hamish.'

'Please.' Hamish nodded, wondering, not for the first time, why emergency nurses *talked* so much as he reached out for the phone when it rang.

'Emergency. Hamish speaking.'

'Hi, Hamish, good to have you back. It's Rita in Pathology here. We were just sent some bloods over—urgent U and Es and triponin level on a forty-eight-year-old named Mark Fylde. I'll give you the UR number, it's—'

'I know the patient,' Hamish interrupted. 'He's the reason I was called early. What's the results?' He reached for a piece of scrap paper and clicked on his pen.

'Sorry…' Rita winced into the phone as she delivered her by now very familiar line. 'We can't run the tests till the right forms are sent up.'

'The guy's having a heart attack,' Hamish snapped. 'Come on, Rita—just run the tests.'

'I—I really can't,' Rita stammered. 'Not without *first* having the correct form. Did you see the new memo that just came down from Admin—?' She didn't get to finish, just held the phone away from her ear as, one hour back from annual leave, Hamish let rip, right in the middle of Emergency, right there where everyone could see…before slamming down the phone and reaching out for a *new* pad and practically gouging out his orders on the *correct* piece of paper.

'I'll get the porter to take it up to the lab now,' Helen said, reaching out her arm, retrieving the form and then stepping back slowly. 'Honestly, Hamish, I've had all my nurses going through every drawer and every cupboard in the place, I've even been through them myself…' She paused as the phone rang, wrote down the message and handed it to Hamish. 'That was Rita—

because it's *you* she's done them, but she's warning you it's the very last time—I'll page Cardiology for you.'

'Got something for the lab?' Mike, the ancient porter, came over and Hamish handed him the form, then, after a moment's thought retrieved it, added the word 'Thanks' and dug out a couple of dollars from the nearly empty pockets of his white coat, which he handed to Mike.

'Could you stop at the vending machine on the way and bung in a bar of chocolate for Rita?'

'I'll go and check the cubicles again for those blessed forms…' Helen started.

'It was my mistake.' Hamish stopped her. 'They were still in my pocket from before my annual leave.'

'Well, then, you'd better get rid of them!'

'Done!'

Dragging in a deep breath to calm down, he got the last dot of Charlotte's fragrance that was still lingering in the air and for the first time in the longest time he wasn't thinking about work, or his son, or any of the other things that usually crowded his mind. Instead, and rather disconcertingly, it was a woman who filled his thoughts.

A woman who wasn't Emma.

Charlotte Porter was the most contrary, confusing person he had ever met, dizzy and happy, yet shrewd and incredibly wise.

Andy was right…

As Helen placed a mug in front of him he snapped to attention, speaking with the cardiologist, then scribbling furiously on the page in front of him, even chatting as Helen bemoaned the bed state and the new computer system. But no matter how he quashed it, no matter how much he attempted to ignore the thought, like a blow—fly it buzzed around him until he acknowledged it and even elaborated...

Charlotte Porter was seriously beautiful.

'Hey!' Many cups of tea and a whole lot of work later, Hamish looked up as his sister knocked and came into his office. 'You're looking very smart.'

'Thanks.'

'No Bailey?' Hamish frowned, peering behind her as if he expected his son to come running towards him, his frown deepening as he realised his sister's usual sunny smile was markedly absent. 'Is he—?'

'Bailey's fine,' Belinda quickly reassured him. 'He's still in crèche—I just wanted to have a quick chat before I head home and think about dinner.'

'No wonder I'm hungry,' Hamish said, glancing up at the clock and grimacing. 'I haven't even had lunch. Bel, can this wait? You can imagine how behind I am—I've been off for two weeks—'

'It can't wait.' Taking a seat at his desk, she sat silent for the longest time, opening her mouth a couple of times to speak then stopping—almost waiting perhaps for Hamish to jump in, to smooth the way, to make this easier.

Only he didn't want to.

It wasn't the mountain of paperwork that had piled up during his absence that made him evasive to her request for a chat—it was the chat itself. Hamish had known this conversation was coming—for the past few days, weeks even, deep down he'd know that this moment would arrive and, like it or not, he had to face it. Staring over at his sister, seeing her anguished expression, his features softened—she'd done so, so much for him this past eighteen months, the very least he could do was help her a little bit here.

Even if he didn't want to.

'Am I right in assuming that the suit you're wearing isn't just because you fancied a change from jeans?'

Biting down on her lip, Belinda nodded.

'And would I be right again if I said that that folder on your lap contained a résumé and some references?'

Staring at his sister, so smart, so efficient-looking, her face made up, her hair beautifully styled, she looked a world away from the jeans-clad and T-shirted housewife and mum he'd been so reliant on recently.

'You're going back to work?'

'I didn't want to say anything till I was sure. I know I should have…'

'You don't have to run your career by me, Belinda—you're a doctor just as much as I am. Of course, once Alicia started back at school you'd be looking to go back.'

'Only part time,' Belinda said quickly. 'I'll be working in Outpatients mainly and doing a few A and E day shifts, a sort of fill-in really… I'll still be able to help loads with Bailey, just…'

'Not as much,' Hamish finished for her. 'It's fine—I'll manage.'

'How?' Belinda's question mirrored exactly what

Hamish was thinking—now was not the time to tell her that Elsie, his faithful but completely past it, live-in housekeeper, thanks to Hamish's pull with the theatre waiting lists, had had her knee construction brought forward to this week. But Belinda, as usual, was two steps ahead of him.

'Elsie's having her knee operation in a couple of days,' Belinda said helplessly. 'And you're always being called in to work at night…'

'I'll sort something out.'

'They want me to start immediately. There's actually a shift they want me to fill tomorrow. I've told them I can't…'

'Well, go back down and tell them that you can,' Hamish said firmly. 'I'll ring the hospital crèche now and extend Bailey's hours…'

'You need more help than just day care, Hamish.'

'Fine—then I'll ring the nanny agency and I'll…' He paused for a moment, trying and failing to fathom how, on top of everything else, he was going to manage to slot in interviewing a live-in nanny for Bailey. And not just conduct interviews—the spare bedroom was more like a store cupboard, in desperate need of decorating…

'I've already found someone.'

'What?' Dragged out of his introspection, Hamish blinked at his sister. 'A nanny?'

'Not a nanny,' Belinda gave a nervous smile. 'It would cost a fortune to have a full-time live-in nanny and there's no need. Bailey's happy here at the hospital crèche—especially with you popping into see him now and then. I'll be able to as well. You just need someone who can share the workload a bit, take him and pick him up when you or I can't, someone to get dinner started, someone who will be there if you're called in at night…'

'And who's going to do all that?' Hamish tried to keep the edge out of his voice. 'I can't employ someone to work two hours here and there…'

'She's a nurse,' Belinda broke in. 'She's got lots of experience with children. I interviewed her this morning. In return for babysitting she gets your spare room…'

'It's a bit more than babysitting…'

'And it's a bit more than just the spare room.' Belinda smiled nervously. 'The stables, too—she comes with a horse and a pony.'

'No!' His response was instant—the conversation absolutely closed—but Belinda was desperate.

'The stables are just sitting there empty, Hamish.'

'Is it any wonder? The *last* thing I want or need now is horses around the place.'

'And the last thing I want is to turn down this job!' She was nearly crying now. 'It's the only way we can do it. Charlotte's just moved from the country, she's staying at the local youth hostel while she tries to find a flat, but on top of rent and everything she can't afford the agistment fees for her animals. I advertised for someone who wanted cheap accommodation but, really, you couldn't charge the girl—she's completely happy to help out properly. She works here, Hamish, and she's more than happy to help with Bailey, to drop him off at crèche and pick him up now and then…'

'Does she know how erratic my hours are?'

'Charlotte's a nurse—she gets it!'

'Charlotte?'

'Charlotte Porter.' Belinda nodded. 'Do you know her? She works here at the hospital.'

'Which is all the more reason that this can't work. I don't want to be living with someone I see each day.'

'So you *do* know her?'

'No,' Hamish said quickly, beating back the image of her breezing into the cubicle.

'I just don't see how it can work.'

'Surely it's worth a try?' Belinda gave a tired smile. 'Hamish, I want to help you all I can, I truly do. With Emma gone, I know how much you need me, and I'm more than happy to pitch in with Bailey. Charlotte gets her shifts four weeks in advance so we can juggle our schedules… I have to go back to work, Hamish.'

'I know.' Hamish nodded but Belinda shook her head.

'No, Hamish, you don't. This isn't just about my career…' Her eyes pleaded for him to listen and she took a deep breath. 'We need the money. Rick's firm's talking about relocating to Melbourne. We're not going.' She shook her head as Hamish's eyes widened. 'Don't worry, we're not going.'

'You have to do what's right by your family, Bel. Don't worry about—'

'You and Bailey are my family, too,' Belinda broke in, 'and aside from that, we don't want to move, we love it here. Rick's even talking about starting up a business on his own—it might even turn out to be a good thing in the long run, but for now there's a real possibility that he could be out of work in a couple of months.'

Despite more than a few clashes with Belinda while they had been growing up, since Hamish had suddenly been widowed, Belinda and her husband Rick had been amazing, had dropped everything and been there through thick and thin with him. Mired in grief, struggling just to get through each day, guiltily Hamish realised he'd never actually stopped to wonder if they had problems of their own. 'Why on earth didn't you tell me this sooner?'

'Because you've got enough problems to deal with without mine.' Standing up, Belinda ended the difficult conversation and braced herself to start the next one—her hand on the door so she could run when the explosion hit! 'Please, give this a go, Hamish. I know it's not ideal but it really could be the best solution for you and Bailey.'

'Nothing is ideal,' Hamish gave a wry smile that didn't meet his eyes—without Emma nothing would ever be perfect again. 'Don't worry about me—things will be fine.'

'You'll give it a go with Charlotte.'

'I'll see.' Hamish refused to be railroaded. 'And, Belinda, if *you* need any help, anything at all, you know I'm here.'

'I know you are,' Belinda replied. 'Please, don't let Rick know I said anything about his work.'

'I won't say a word. So when does this Charlotte move in? I suppose I should ring a decorator…'

'No need.' Belinda winced as she opened his office door. 'She's moving in as we speak. I know I should have run it by you first, but she was just so perfect I gave her the job there and then.'

'You what?' His voice was like a whip cracking. 'You had no right—'

'Perhaps,' Belinda interrupted, 'but I would never have taken this job without first finding a viable solution for you and Bailey. I just never expected it to happen so quickly—if I hadn't met Charlotte myself I would never even have considered resuming work so soon.'

'I decide who looks after my son—I decide who I share my home with—so you can go and tell this Charlotte—'

Belinda had known it wouldn't be that easy—instead of bolting out of the door, she closed it and, walking to his desk, said the toughest words of her life.

'Fine. But on my way out of here I *am* going down to Admin to tell them I can do that shift tomorrow.' She watched as his jaw tightened and felt like the biggest bitch in the world as she continued—but Hamish had to realise just how urgent the situation was. 'Oh, and Elsie's niece rang this morning—suggested the old girl might like to spend a couple of days with her before the operation and recuperate there afterwards. 'I thought about saying no, of course…that you were on call tomorrow night…'

'You didn't—did you?'

'Of course not.' Belinda sniffed as she looked over to her brother, wished for the millionth time that his life wasn't just so *hard*, her voice way softer when she next spoke.

'Look, Hamish, sometimes opportunities come and you have to grab them. You trust me to make the right choices for you and Bailey don't you?' Belinda asked, waiting till Hamish gave a reluctant, tense nod. 'I placed an ad in yesterday's local paper, I thought it would be the first step in an exhausting process. I was actually going to speak to you tonight then out of the blue Charlotte rang. I told her to come over this morning, which she did, and Bailey fell in love with her on the spot. She's quite amazing actually.' Belinda gave a small laugh. 'She'd just finished a night shift, though you'd never have guessed. Instead of crashing, she's moving her stuff in and sorting out the spare room and heading off to the hardware store for some sample paint pots!'

'What if I'd said no?' Hamish stared at his sister. 'What if—?'

'You couldn't say no,' his sister pointed out. 'Something had to change. Like it or not, Hamish, we all need help sometimes.' Her heart twisted as finally, reluctantly, her very proud brother nodded. 'Do you want me to pick up Bailey and give him dinner? Then we can all head to your place and I'll introduce you to Charlotte—assuming she's awake, that is.'

Staring at the mountain of paperwork, Hamish was again about to say yes, to accept, whether he liked it or not, that he needed help, that it would be great if she could pick up Bailey and give him dinner…

Again.

An image of his son's face flashed before his eyes so vivid, so tangible, he could *see* him, could smell that baby scent still buried within the soft two-year-old's curls, could see those fat rosy cheeks glowing, two pudgy little hands reaching out to be picked up...

He'd been a father for two years—but in the last two weeks Hamish had actually become a dad.

Two treasured weeks where he'd taken some long overdue annual leave—and for the first time he'd actually stopped to draw breath since Emma had died. For the first time in what seemed like for ever his day hadn't constituted an endless logistical nightmare, trying to combine a demanding career with a two-year-old, juggling day care with his roster and night calls with his eternally patient sister and Elsie, trying to remember to pay the bills, Elsie's and the gardener's wages, to make time for Bailey—oh, yes, and to occasionally remember to eat!

Instead, during his leave he'd discovered the bliss of long lie-ins—Bailey clambering in bed beside him, fun DVDs and even funnier attempts at dancing and singing into a plastic microphone, waiting for Bailey, dressed in nothing more than a T-shirt, to please just wee into the shiny red potty that Hamish had recently bought.

Bailey hadn't.

Not once.

The house reeked of antiseptic, there were little scrubbed patches on a hundred places on the carpet, as if there were a new puppy in the house—and he'd loved every minute.

As vital as his work was, right now, staring at admission cards and letters of complaint, the paperwork for a drug trial he was conducting and the 'urgent response' that was required to the CEO's latest budget slash, Hamish just didn't care. The only place he wanted to be was with his son—everything else would just have to wait.

'You go home, Bel—I'll pick up Bailey.'

'You're sure?' Belinda checked, frowning at the pensive note in his voice. 'Look, Hamish, if me going back to work—'

'This isn't about you going back to work,' Hamish interrupted, and something in his voice must have told Belinda he meant it, something in his voice stopped her defensive approach, her eyes welling with tears of understanding as for the millionth she pondered her brother's plight. 'It's about Bailey being pushed from pillar to post just so that I can keep doing this job.'

'You love your job.'

Do I? Hamish asked himself. Oh, sure, he *had* loved it, knew that he was good at it, knew that now more than ever, with all the changes in the hospital, he was very heavily needed, but with every day that passed, with every morning drop-off at crèche or middle of the night drop-offs at Belinda, he resented it a little bit more.

For his son's sake.

'In a few years Bailey will be at school,' Belinda pointed out. 'Things will get so much easier then.'

Hazel eyes stared back at her, the only colour in his pale face.

'And that's his baby years gone.' Hamish didn't say anything more, he didn't have to, grateful for Belinda's nod of understanding, grateful that she didn't come up with any platitude that might gloss over the simple fact that, yes, Belinda had been great and, sure, Charlotte might get them through the next couple of months while Elsie recovered from her operation, but he was tired of getting by, and not just for him…

After a quick check and update with his doctors Hamish walked up to the child-care centre, pressing the intercom to enter, his heart twisting as he saw his little boy. Clearly tired, Bailey was curled up on one of the low sofas, half watching the early evening movie that was put on for children whose parents worked late.

Bailey could recite the words to each one.

Hazel eyes met hazel.

Strange, Hamish thought as he signed the register and headed over to his son, how delighted Emma had been to produce a 'mini-Hamish'. The same jet hair, the same pale skin, the same colour eyes, though as beautiful as his son was, sometimes, at moments like this, he wished he looked more like his mother.

Wished there was just a little bit more of his beautiful Emma left in the world for him to hold onto.

CHAPTER TWO

WHO would have thought the colour white could be so complicated?

Standing back, watching as the late afternoon sun transformed the six squares she had painted on the wall, Charlotte was torn with indecision—each and every shade of white taking on an entirely different hue as the sun bobbed ever lower, glaring through the window and drenching the dank room she was attempting to rapidly and very cheaply transform.

White bedspread, white muslin on the windows, white *everything*, Charlotte had decided, only why where there so-o many shades?

But it wasn't her colour scheme, or lack of it, that was the problem, Charlotte admitted, glancing at her faithful alarm clock and realising that at any moment Hamish would be home.

Not for a second when she'd met him that morning had it even entered her head that her dream accommodation might mean sharing a house with him.

Professional father of one requires help with some

irregular babysitting duties in return for reduced-cost
accommodation.

Rural property—set on acreage—animals welcome.
Need to be flexible.
Experience with children essential.
Contact Belinda.

It had seemed like a dream come true. Her heart in her mouth, Charlotte had rung the given number, hope mounting as Belinda had cheerfully waved away Charlotte's problem of the relocation of her beloved horses from the country—had assured her that her little menagerie wouldn't be a problem.

There *had* to be a catch, Charlotte had decided as she had driven her ancient car up the driveway of Adams farm for her interview and had glimpsed the gorgeous sprawling property, nearly swooning on her animals' behalf at the sight of acre after acre of lush grass, courtesy of a dam and efficient irrigation system. But most importantly of all, she'd promptly melted as Belinda had guided her into the kitchen, a massive family room set behind it, and on the sofa in the middle a delicious two-year-old who had happily climbed all over her the second she had sat down.

And then, just as she'd predicted, she'd found out the catch! Approximately two minutes into the conversation all the little snippets of information she'd gleaned about Hamish since working in the emergency department had fallen into place—mind you, detective school wasn't a prerequisite to work out there surely weren't *that* many widowed accident and emergency consultants named Hamish living in the area!

'His regular housekeeper is being admitted to

hospital for a knee reconstruction—she's just gone to spend a couple of days with her niece,' Belinda explained, 'and I've just been offered a job that, frankly, I can't afford to turn down.'

'Shouldn't Hamish at least meet me first?' Charlotte asked. 'I mean, if we're going to be living together, if I'm going to be looking after his child.'

'Bailey would be eighteen years old and driving if I left it to Hamish to find someone he considered suitable! Look, Charlotte, when I put in this advertisement I never dreamt someone as suitable as you would come along... And just look at Bailey.' She smiled fondly at her nephew, bouncing up and down on Charlotte's knee as if he'd known her all his life. 'I'll talk to Hamish—you just let me know how soon you can move in.'

'I'm staying at the local youth hostel.' Charlotte blushed, wondering if that fact alone would be enough to jinx her chances. 'Just till I find somewhere.'

'Well, guess what?' Belinda smiled. 'You just did!'

Despite Belinda being so sure she could get Hamish to agree, Charlotte felt the knot in her stomach tighten when she heard a car crunch along the gravel, wondering how the rather terse Hamish Adams she had met that morning would have reacted to the news that his sister had in a matter of hours found him a live-in babysitter who just happened to work alongside him.

Oh, God!

Feeling the butterflies leaping like salmon in her stomach, her hand clenching so hard on the paintbrush that shades of orchid white seeped through her fingers, Charlotte caught a glimpse of herself in the bedroom mirror.

What would Cassie have done in a situation like this?

It was a question she asked herself ten, sometimes a hundred times a day.

Whenever she was unsure, whenever she couldn't quite work out how to deal with a particular scenario, Charlotte tried to work out what her big sister by eight and half minutes would do, and more often that not the answer was the same: Cassie wouldn't give two hoots!

She smiled and the butterflies in her stomach settled just a fraction. Why, Cassie wouldn't even notice the awkwardness of the moment—she'd just swan down the stairs with a wide smile and talk her walk through any strained silence.

With lipstick on!

After wiping her hands on her already woefully paint-stained jeans, Charlotte rummaged in her bag and pulled out the necessary props to turn her pale, strained lips into a pretty pink pout then squirted the remaining dregs of her perfume onto her neck before taking a deep breath and marching out her very new bedroom door.

'Hamish!' Descending the stairs, her smile stayed firmly intact as, without even glancing up, he deposited his laptop, a bag of groceries, a nappy bag and then finally his gorgeous son onto the hallway floor. 'Fancy meeting you here!'

'Fancy!' Hamish said dryly, before deigning a glance at her. 'So I was the interview you were dashing off to?'

'Seems that way.' Her heart in her mouth and absolutely refusing to show it, Charlotte neglected the remaining few steps and stood a good a few inches above him—grateful for the diversion of a pudgy, happy toddler emptying the contents of his nappy bag over the hall floor. Anything was easier than looking at Hamish right now. 'I really had no idea this morning it was you I'd be…'

'Living with,' Hamish finished for her, without ending the sentence, and internally Charlotte blanched as he continued, 'working with, sharing child care with.'

'It might seem a touch awkward at first…' Charlotte attempted, but gave in there—nothing was going to thaw the strained atmosphere in the hall. The rather irritable but kind doctor she had encountered that morning was light years from the forebidding-looking man who was glaring at her now, and suddenly the haven she'd found for her animals, the glimpse at *finally* getting her finances in order, all faded into the distance.

'Awkward doesn't come close,' Hamish muttered, flicking on the light and stomping down the hall, but checking himself at the sight of her crestfallen face he relented a touch. 'It's not you I'm annoyed with, there's just no way this can possibly work.' Hamish interrupted her thoughts as if he knew them. 'Belinda should have spoken to me. Have you already booked the transport for your horses?'

She didn't even bother to correct him, just gave a nervous nod. 'A friend has to pick up his new horse from somewhere near here in a couple of weeks—he's going to bring them down, along with the last of my boxes…' Her voice trailed off as he opened his mouth to speak. Clearly he was about to tell her to cancel it but the seal and signature on the death warrant was momentarily halted by a delighted squeal of recognition from Bailey as, nappy bag completely empty, he'd looked for the next distraction and, catching sight of Charlotte in the hall for the first time since he'd come home, he actually looked at her, so excited to see her he didn't even stand, just scrambled along the hallway in a curious impersonation of a crawl and held out his arms to be picked up.

'He seems to like you.'

'Why wouldn't he?' Charlotte answered, scooping him up, 'I'm friendly, house-trained…'

'Look,' Hamish broke in irritably, 'I'm sure you're great, but this simply can't work. People will think that…' Hazel eyes held hers as his voice trailed off but Charlotte stared boldly back.

'That were having a steamy, torrid affair?' Now, *that* really was Cassie speaking, but when she was rewarded with the tiniest of tiny smiles, Charlotte was brave enough to continue in her own voice. 'I know it must be horribly awkward for you. I'm sure that since you lost your wife your personal life has been fodder for everyone you work with. However, I'm incredibly discreet.' To that point he had appeared slightly mollified, but his questioning eyebrow prompted insistence. 'I *am* discreet—I might chat about everything and nothing to anyone, but I would never talk about things that matter.'

'Whether you do or not— Who the hell is that?' His response was terminated as Charlotte's faithful cat padded down the stairs behind her, mewing loudly and blinking with sleep-filled eyes, clearly bemused as to what all the fuss was about.

'That's Maisy.' Charlottes smile was finally genuine. 'He's my kitten.'

'That's no kitten!' Hamish stared in astonishment at the rather oversized feline. 'It's a bloody lion. It's huge!'

'He's a ragdoll cat—and he hasn't finished growing yet! My mum used to breed them—this one was the last of her last litter!'

He did yet another double-take. 'Isn't Maisy a girl's name?'

"I thought he was a she—the name just sort of stuck.'

'And I thought you just had two horses.'

'One horse,' Charlotte corrected, 'and a pony. Fitz is the horse—Scottie's the pony.'

'Any other animal I should know about, apart from the horse and pony and the kitten with a gender identity crisis?' His sarcasm was replaced with resignation as a dizzy cocker spaniel fled down the stairs.

'Just Eric.'

'Eric is a boy, I assume?'

'Of course.' Charlotte grinned. 'Why on earth would I call a girl Eric?' Her brave smile faded as he stared back at her then, almost imperceptibly, shook his head, and she knew what was coming, could see his mouth opening to deliver the words she so badly didn't want to hear.

'Maybe you should hold off on bringing down the horses....' Hamish stood firm as her world again crumbled. 'I'm not going to throw you out on the street or anything but...'

'You just don't want me getting too at home.'

'Exactly.'

'Could we have a trial period?' She hated begging, hated it more than anything, but she literally had no choice. 'Look, I need this to work.'

'Why?'

'Because I'm broke,' Charlotte answered honestly. 'Because—as you've seen—I've got a menagerie demanding that I provide them with a home, and I'm certainly not going to jeopardise that by telling anyone who cares to listen that you snore at night or don't put the loo seat down.'

The wariness, the coolness in those proud dark eyes diminished just a touch as Bailey squeezed the life out of her neck and attempted her name.

'Dar-dot!'

'You seem to have made a bit of hit there.'

'So has Bailey,' Charlotte said simply. 'He's adorable.'

But Hamish wasn't about to be forced into anything. Instead, after only the briefest of hesitations he walked past her and headed towards the kitchen.

'I'd better get some dinner on for Bailey—oh, and can you make sure the pets stay downstairs? I don't want that lion climbing into his cot.'

'Sure. And I've already made dinner,' Charlotte said, watching as he jerked his head in surprise. 'Just lamb and potatoes…' She followed him through to the kitchen, standing just behind him as he stared at the neatly laid kitchen table—the rather dusty highchair she had found against the wall gleaming in pride of place. 'Elsie said she'd stocked you up enough to see the week out. I'll just pop some peas in the microwave and it should be ready in a couple of moments. Bailey does like lamb, doesn't he?'

'I'm not sure.' For once it was Hamish who sounded embarrassed.

'Only Elsie said there was some in the freezer.' Her hands shaking and trying not to show it, she clumsily served up, spilling gravy all over the bench—not that Hamish noticed. He was too busy trying to pry a tired unyielding body into the highchair she'd set up.

'He's not used to it.' Hamish gave an almost apologetic shrug as Charlotte bought a bowel over and placed it in font of Bailey. 'It's normally chicken nuggets or fish fingers and frozen chips over there at the coffee table in the family room.'

'I'm not used to it either,' Charlotte admitted. 'It took me about five goes just to set the highchair up!'

'But Belinda said you had a lot of experience with children!"

'With sick ones I've had loads,' Charlotte said distractedly, missing his appalled expression, 'but healthy ones like this little honey are a complete enigma to me. I guess we'll have to work it out together—won't we Bailey?'

Bailey was giggling so much as she tickled him that he forgot to refuse the teaspoon she'd laden with finely chopped meat and mash and peas all swilling in gravy—his giggles fading as everyone present, Bailey included, found out that he did like lamb after all. And not only that, he could eat without help from Hamish or Charoltte! His little hand eagerly grabbed the spoon from Charlotte and then messily shovelled his dinner into his mouth.

'On your meat or potatoes?'

'Sorry?'

Pan poised, Charlotte made herself clearer as Hamish stared in amazement at his son. 'Do you like your gravy on your meat or potatoes?'

'Whatever.'

Despite the fairly good start, it was the most strained of strained dinners.

Far worse than any first date—far worse than some embarrassing set-up by friends or a blind date for the hell of it.

This one had the added cringe factor of being an unwelcome guest in the man's home with no waiter or wine list or the hum of fellow diners to break the appalling silence. Even Bailey let both sides down—contentedly chewing his dinner then promptly deserting the sinking ship by falling asleep at the table, his dark curls awash with gravy and potatoes, one hand clutching his teaspoon, his little thumb on his other hand stuck firmly in his mouth.

'How come you suddenly need somewhere for all your animals?' It was Hamish who finally gave in.

'My mum's moving up to Queensland,' Charlotte answered.

'How come she's moving?'

'She's got a new boyfriend.' Charlotte smiled as Hamish frowned. 'And I mean *boyfriend*! He's not much older than me!'

'Oh!'

'Still, he seems to make her happy.'

'You get on well?'

'I haven't met him yet.' Charlotte shrugged. 'Mum met him on holiday a few months back—it's been one of those whirlwind romances. Apparently he lives in one of those gorgeous high-rise apartments overlooking the ocean—which doesn't leave much room for the pets.'

'But if you lived at home, couldn't you have stayed there for a while?'

'There's no more work. The local hospital closed last month—about the same time Mum told me that she wanted to sell up and move. I'm packing up the house for her—it sold last week.'

'So you're stuck with the pets.'

'Hardly stuck.' Charlotte smiled. 'They're all mine—it's hardly fair to expect Mum to miss out on the man of her dreams because of my pets.'

'I guess,' Hamish answered, only he wasn't quite convinced. Selling up the family home and leaving her daughter to not only find work but homes for the pets as well, seemed more than just a touch selfish, irresponsible even. Not that Charlotte seemed to think so—she seemed genuinely delighted for her mother.

'What about your father?' Hamish asked, growing more curious by the minute.

'I don't really see him that much since he walked out.' Charlotte answered factually, while adding another generous dash of gravy to her lamb. 'He had an affair. Well, two, actually, but the second one he kept!'

Maybe irresponsibility ran in the family!

Staring over at her, Hamish tried to fathom her age. Twenty-four or -five perhaps, he thought, glancing at her pretty snub nose, but from the way she'd spoken to young Andy that morning and from what Helen had said about her she certainly wasn't wet behind the ears, yet she'd lived at home for ever and hadn't saved a cent—had been living at the local youth hostel and, from what he'd seen in the driveway, drove an absolute bomb of a car.

Was she really the type of person he wanted looking after Bailey?

Yes!

The answer was there before he'd even finished asking himself the question, his mind flicking back to Andy that morning and the tenderness he'd witnessed when she'd spoken with the troubled little boy. And it wasn't just Andy who adored her, Hamish recalled the sheer incredulous delight on his son's face when he'd greeted her for the second time—and it had nothing to do with Bailey being used to strangers. Despite a seemingly never-ending stream of carers—despite endless people flitting in and out his life—true to the saying that familiarity bred contempt, Bailey was sure that every new face meant a kiss goodbye from his father.

Only not when he'd met Charlotte.

He'd never seen his son so confident with a stranger,

had never seen him so completely at ease with someone he barely knew.

'So there's only you?' Hamish asked, a tiny frown forming as he watched her hand still around the glass of water she was holding. 'No brothers or sisters to help you out?'

'No!' The addition to his sentence allowed her to answer his question honestly, well, sort of…

Even thirteen years on, she still didn't know when was right time to tell someone about Cassie.

Even thirteen years on she still couldn't manage to casually slot into the conversation the most vital piece of her life without breaking down.

How exactly *was* she supposed to say it?

'Oh, I had a twin, identical actually…' or maybe a more casual 'My sister died when she was fifteen…' or… What did one say? For Charlotte it was an endless conundrum—there was *no* easy way of doing it, no way of tossing that little gem into an already awkward conversation. There never had been, or ever would be, a *right* way to reveal her very core. It was easier to just let the moment pass.

And pass it did.

With agonising slowness as Hamish stared over the table at her, trying hard to find a reason not to like her and failing dismally.

'We'd have to set a few house rules,' Hamish said sternly as Charlotte chewed on a piece of lamb that had turned to dust. 'A lot of house rules, actually.'

'Absolutely.' Taking a huge swig of water, she tried not to appear too keen as he thankfully changed the subject and an unexpected glimmer of hope appeared on the horizon.

'I mean, for this to work it would mean a lot of give and take on both sides.'

'Of course.'

'And rule number one is—you use the four-wheel-drive.'

'Sorry?'

'A lot of the roads around here aren't sealed—it would be far safer for you in the Jeep.'

'I'm quite capable of controlling a vehicle—'

'I don't care how capable a driver you are—you are *not* driving Bailey around in that bomb you have parked in the driveway. And given that the whole point of this exercise is that you can pick up and drop off Bailey now and then—and sometimes at short notice—I'd prefer it if you used the Jeep while you're here.'

'Ooh, I can live with that!' Charlotte grinned. After all it was hardly a hardship—a blessing actually. She desperately needed new tyres! It seemed she was staying. Now she just needed to get to know the elusive Hamish. 'So how *have* you managed?' she asked, a trace of sympathy softening the directness of her question.

'Excuse me?'

'Belinda said that your wife died when Bailey was six months old. I was just wondering how you managed to hold down such a demanding job *and* raise a little one.'

He stared across at the table, taken back by the directness of her question. In the eighteen months he'd been a widower no one had actually asked him.

'I don't know how you manage!' was an almost daily observation, along with the infinitely annoying: *'I just couldn't cope if it happened to me…'* As if he somehow had a choice *but* to cope. Sure, he'd had endless help from his sister and, till now, Elsie, but for Charlotte, for someone he'd known less than a day, to actually ask him *how* he did it all was confronting, yet strangely refreshing.

'With great difficulty.' Hamish answered the direct question with a very honest answer. 'Both demand a great deal and both merit a lot more attention than I'm able to give them.'

There—he'd said it! Taking a drink of water, Hamish realised he'd actually admitted to another human being what he hardly dared think himself—not that he expected her to come up with an answer, not that he expected the conversation to go any further. It was just so nice to actually talk, to sit with another adult at the end of a long and difficult day and share a little of what was on his mind.

Only he didn't yet know Charlotte.

'Well, this little guy's not going anywhere.' Charlotte dug a spoon into her potato and smeared it around her plate, soaking up the last of her gravy like a ten-year-old would while offering the opinion of someone far wiser. 'So that leaves a big question mark over your work. Have you thought about changing jobs?'

Hamish held his water in his mouth for a long time before swallowing. 'To what?'

'I'll have to think about that one.' She smiled across the table at him and it was somehow as if she actually understood, somehow *knew* the pain that was locked inside him. For an incredible second she wasn't a stranger, wasn't yet another necessary intruder in the chaos his life had become since Emma's tragic death.

Bailey's spoon, which he had been clutching in his free hand, clattered noisily to the floor as he crept deeper into slumber, breaking the bizarre moment.

'Seems a shame to wake him to bath him,' Hamish said gruffly, embarrassed by his revelation, stunned at his own thought process and just wanting to get the hell out of there. 'Still, I won't have time in the morning and can hardly send him off to day care with his hair stuck together.'

'Leave him here, then.' Charlotte shrugged. 'He can watch me paint.'

'Er, two-year-olds and paintbrushes aren't the best combination. Anyway, that's a lot more than a casual babysit. Tomorrow's your day off.'

'I don't mind,' Charlotte said honestly. 'It would be really nice to get to know him.'

'You see…' Hamish was chasing his peas around his plate, clearly not comfortable with asking for help. 'I'm actually on call tomorrow night. If we are going to give this a trial, I was actually hoping, if you weren't going out, or if you didn't have a date or anything, that maybe you could listen out for him. I can't promise he won't wake, though, as he's teething at the moment. But I don't always get called in.'

'Fine.' Charlotte nodded. 'Just knock and let me know if you do get called so that I can listen out for him.'

'You're sure?'

'Completely.'

'Right.' With supreme gentleness he scooped Bailey out of his highchair, cuddled the exhausted little boy into his broad chest. 'I'll give him a quick bath—if you could have listen out for him tomorrow night—'

'Hamish,' Charlotte interrupted. 'Surely if there's a chance I might be getting up to him tomorrow night then I should spend some time during the day with him. I mean it—I'd love to have him tomorrow.'

He was about to say no, but feeling the exhausted weight of his son in his arms, the thought of just laying him down in his cot, of letting him *just* sleep, had a slightly bemused Hamish not answering, just heading upstairs to Bailey's bedroom.

Staring down at him, his face messy, his hair a matted mess of potato and a dreamy smile on his lips, Hamish envisaged heading downstairs and not having to pack the nappy bag for tomorrow, for one luxurious day not having to wake up a fretful little boy at the crack of dawn because his dad had to go to work. It was just too tempting not to head down the stairs and back to the kitchen to say yes to Charlotte's generous offer.

He didn't even make it to the top of the stairs. 'Thank you very much, Charlotte, if you're sure. I know Bailey would love to spend the day at home.'

'No problem. We'll have fun. 'Night, then!' Charlotte beamed.

'You're going to bed?' He frowned at his watch. 'It's only seven-thirty.'

'I've been up for twenty-four hours,' Charlotte

pointed out. 'Just give me a knock when you leave—perhaps open my bedroom door so I can hear him.'

'Sure.'

'I've left the dishes for you to do.' Charlotte smothered a yawn then gave an impish smile. 'I cooked so you wash up—house rule number two!'

'Fair enough—good night, Charlotte! Sleep well!'

Never, when he'd said it that morning, had Hamish thought he'd be saying it again to her just twelve hours later.

And never had he envisaged doing the dishes tonight. Usually there were just the two plates he and Bailey had eaten their ready-prepared meals off.

Well, not really the dishes, but even stacking the dishwasher usually seemed like a mammoth task. There was always so much to do—always a stack of work he'd bought home, Bailey to feed and bathe, his bag to be packed for day care. It was just easier to leave the dishes for Elsie or put them off till the next day. But by eight o'clock the dishwasher was whirring, Bailey was fast asleep and most surprisingly of all there were no baked beans for Hamish's supper turning in the microwave. In fact, there was *nothing* he really had to do!

'Hamish…' Charlotte poked her head around the doorway, making him jump, especially when he caught more than a glimpse of a naked, creamy white shoulder, naked because the extremely thin strap of her nightdress was halfway down her arm. 'You could lecture.'

'Sorry?'

'Teach medicine—to med students. There'd be no night-shift callouts, you'd get all the school holidays off, which might not seem important now, but in a few years' time…' He was staring at her as if she was speaking a foreign language, and she realised he had no idea what she was referring to. 'What we were talking about at the dinner table about you finding a more Bailey-friendly job.'

'Oh, that?' Hamish scratched his head and actually thought about it for a second. 'I hate teaching, well, in a formal setting, although I suppose I don't mind when it's hands on. I don't think I'd be very patient but, yep, it's certainly worth a thought.'

'Just an idea.' Charlotte smiled, disappearing from view and still talking. 'I'll have another think for you—I'm sure I can come up with something!'

'Er, thanks,' he called to the closing door.

Teaching?

When he'd told her his problem he'd never thought she'd actually come up with an answer—and a good one, too. Not that he could see himself teaching but, still, it was food for thought.

Padding around the house for the first time in the longest time, unsure of what to do with his first real free time in months, Hamish consulted the TV guide then, perhaps wisely, realising Bailey would make up for his golden behavior tonight in a few short hours, he bypassed the television for the sheer luxury of a quick shower and an inordinately early night, waking up, if not refreshed, at least semi-conscious when Bailey's erupting teeth made their presence known around two in the morning.

Tiptoeing past Charlotte's room, with his hand

gently over a roaring Bailey's mouth as he tried not to wake her, it was *impossible* not to be aware of her presence as he gave his son a cool drink, changed his nappy and then attempted to cuddle him back to sleep…*impossible* not to sit on the sofa and stare into the darkness and try to fathom how his life had changed in the twelve hours since Charlotte Porter had breezed into his world.

CHAPTER THREE

AND how it changed!

Within in a matter of days the spare room was painted, the dog and cat had commandeered the sofa, the bathroom sink was barely accessible thanks to a mountain of make-up and fragrance bottles and, for Hamish, most difficult of all was trying not to notice the tiny, tiny, brightly coloured knickers constantly blowing on the clothesline, which was visible from a kitchen where the radio seemed permanently on.

Charlotte was very firmly *in situ*!

'Charlotte!'

Waking up to her name and the smell of paint, Charlotte flicked on her bedside light and waited for a face to appear around her bedroom door, but instead it was the door that spoke, sounding incredibly like Hamish!

'I'm really sorry to wake you up, only I have to go into work.'

'That's fine.' Charlotte yawned. 'I'll listen out in case Bailey wakes up.'

'That's the problem—he's been up for the last hour.' On cue, Bailey let out a grizzle. 'Look, it's not an urgent call-in, you don't have to rush…'

'It's really no problem!'

She appeared moments later in the kitchen dressed in nothing more than a white cotton nightdress, a huge pillow crease on her face and blinking at the mess that had been created in the couple of hours since she'd gone to bed—the contents of Bailey's nappy bag were strewn across the floor, and the coffee table was littered with various cups and baby bottles.

'He's teething,' Hamish explained, pacing the floor with a fretful Bailey. 'Normally you wouldn't even have to get up at all—when he isn't teething he sleeps right through. I don't know what he wants!'

'A new set of gums, perhaps. Poor little thing…' She pouted at Bailey and held out her arms to him. Amazingly he stopped crying but, just a little bit shy, just a little bit coy, he lowered his head back into his dad's neck.

'You didn't have to race down.' Hamish gave a small cough, trying and failing not to notice the very thin spaghetti straps on her nightdress, which looked as if they might snap against the strain of her—very clearly minus a bra—bosom. 'You can go and, er, put on a dressing gown or something and I'll make you a coffee.'

'I don't own a dressing gown…' Charlotte yawned. 'And I don't want a coffee at this hour—it will keep me up.'

'That's the intention,' Hamish said dryly, gesturing to the coffee table and feeling miffed and pleased at the same time when, on the second offer of a cuddle, Bailey happily deserted him. 'You're sure you'll be okay? You can call me on my mobile and Belinda's number's on the fridge.'

'Have you tried an ice-lolly?'

'Sorry?'

'For his gums,' Charlotte said patiently, staring at Bailey's red face and dribbling sore mouth.

'Does that help?'

'I've no idea,' Charlotte admitted. 'But it seems logical!'

He left them sitting on sofa, both sucking on lemonade-flavoured ice-lollies—and, yes, Hamish admitted, maybe it did make sense. Only there was nothing logical about his thoughts as he drove to the hospital!

He was thirty-five years old, for goodness' sake! With a child and a mortgage and an endlessly demanding job—bogged down with responsibility and exhaustion—an impetuous thing like Charlotte wouldn't even *entertain*... He stopped his thought pattern right there before it went any further. In a desperate attempt to distract himself, Hamish rang through to the hospital and chatted with the resident about the problem patient.

A thirty-year-old male who the resident was pretty sure was putting on an impressive act in an attempt to get some drugs.

'I think I know him,' Hamish said. 'I've come across him before—just tell him you need a second opinion before you can give him any pain medication. I'll be there in five.'

* * *

One look at Hamish's rather familiar and less than impressed face and the patient knew he'd been rumbled, quickly jumping off the gurney and getting dressed at full speed then adding a few expletives for good measure as he raced out of the department as Hamish watched without uttering a single word.

'Sorry to drag you in,' Cameron addressed his boss. 'He came in under a false name, so I didn't know that you'd already seen him.'

'Several times.' Hamish nodded. 'And don't be sorry for calling me in—you did well to pick up that he was lying. He had me fooled once.'

'Really?' Cameron said doubtfully. Hamish Adams rarely got things wrong.

'Well, nearly. Is there anything else you need me for before I head home?'

'Nope, we're pretty quiet. Hopefully I won't have to wake you again.'

'With the way Bailey's behaving at the moment, I somehow don't think it'll be you waking me.'

Only this time he was wrong...

Letting himself into the house, expecting chaos, or at least a bordering-on hysterical Bailey, he frowned at the darkness, flicking on the kitchen light, and it was as if the fairies had whizzed in in the short time he had been away as he stared at the relatively tidy family room. Bailey's bag had been repacked and stood ready to go in the morning, cups and bottles washed and draining, and most surprisingly of all the delightful sound of silence.
DELEGATE!!!!!!!!!!!!

He saw the bold word written on Bailey's chalk board and smiled as he picked up a piece of chalk, thinking of her scribbling it before she'd gone to bed—the chalk board Charlotte's newest tool in communication as she endlessly came up with suggestions to help his work situation. She'd run the gamut—had even had him considering ascending, or metaphorically descending, the miserable stairs to a senior advisory role in hospital admin.

She was right—he should delegate more. There were three consultants in the place so why did everyone, when it was urgent (and given the nature of his job it usually was!) always end up calling him?

Hamish knew the answer. Picking up the chalk, he revealed it to Charlotte.

'Already tried that—only no one does it as good as me!' he wrote, then changed his mind, deciding that his words might possibly be misconstrued as a bit, well, suggestive! Carefully he rubbed out 'it' and changed it to 'my job', then headed upstairs, passing first Charlotte's bedroom, the door slightly ajar, and, after pausing for just a fraction, heading to Bailey's.

Staring down at his son, seeing the flushed, tear-streaked face he had said goodbye to pale and peaceful, his sore mouth now relaxed in sleep, Hamish knew, with the relief only a frazzled parent could know, that he was out for the count, that a couple of hours of serious sleep were possibly about to ensue…and he wasn't thinking about Bailey!

Heading to bed, still dressed in his theatre gear just in case he was called back in, Hamish actually got under the covers instead of crashing on top and then was afforded the rare luxury of sleeping through the precious remains of the night.

CHAPTER FOUR

'How long till he gets here?'

Slightly breathless from running from day care and ten minutes before his day officially started, Hamish slammed into the resuscitation room with his pager still shrilling urgently to alert him to the incoming emergency and started pulling the necessary equipment off the wall in preparation for the patient.

'Two minutes!' Charlotte answered without looking up, too busy pulling up drugs for the imminent arrival of the patient.

A man had been electrocuted at work and was on his way into the department, and everyone present, from porter to consultant, was racing to do their bit to ensure that this unlucky young man was afforded every possible chance when he presented in the department.

'What do we know?'

'Twenty-eight-year-old male in full cardiac arrest. Electrocution. CPR was commenced by his father—he was intubated at the scene by the paramedics.'

'How long has he been down?'

'Forty minutes from when we got there!' the paramedic answered, bagging the patient with one hand, his face red with exertion as he and his partner sped the ambulance stretcher into Resus, cardiac massage being delivered now by Cameron, the resident. 'Vince, his dad, was on the scene, but we could barely get a word out of him. No response to drugs or defibrillation—he's in fine VF.'

'Do we have a name for the patient?'

'Ronan. Ronan King.'

'Right, let's get him over,' Hamish said, giving the count. 'Cameron, keep up the CPR till we get him onto our monitors…' Connecting the ambu-bag to the wall source of oxygen, Hamish bagged Ronan himself as he listened for air entry with his stethoscope, checking that the tube was correctly positioned. Nodding, he handed over the important job to Charlotte's fellow emergency nurse, Amy. Charlotte connected the unlucky man to the hospital's monitors and other staff ripped through Roman's heavy clothing with scissors, tossing the shredded garments into bags, pulling off his gumboots and alerting Hamish to two nasty burns on Ronan's feet.

'Sats ninety-four percent!' Charlotte called out, relaying every bit of information as it flicked on the screen, while still pulling up drugs into a kidney dish, leaving the ends of the needles in the ampoules to ensure the contents of each vial but allowing for rapid delivery when the doctor requested them.

'Good job, guys,' Hamish acknowledged. That the patient's oxygenation at this dire stage was so good showed the effectiveness of the resuscitation he had been given by the paramedics—but it was what had happened prior to their arrival that was vital, that might well determine the eventual outcome for this young man. And everyone present knew it, but the paramedics didn't even have time to accept his praise, their radios already crackling into life and demanding they move onto their next patient. 'Pupils are fixed and dilated,' Hamish said, shining a light into his patient's eyes but nodding as the paramedic hastily reeled off the drugs that had so far been administered while he collected the equipment as his partner raced out to prepare the ambulance for their next call. Fixed and dilated pupils were an ominous sign of brain injury but atropine had been amongst the medications that had been given—a strong cardiac drug, it also had the effect of fixed and dilated pupils and allowed for the fateful sign to be temporarily ignored.

'Hold the massage and let's see what we've got.' Hamish stared over at the monitor, his hand on the patient's neck, straining to feel a carotid pulse as the monitor faded into fine VF. While the massage was being delivered strong green blips had formed on the screen, a femoral pulse felt, as a strong output was achieved, but as soon as it was halted, as soon as the heart was left to its own devices, just a fine irregular line was all to show for the heart flickering erratically inside.

Yet as dire as it was, there was still hope.

The fact that the heart was still, after all this time, offering some activity, as opposed to the dreaded flat line of aystlole, meant that this resuscitation attempt wasn't anywhere near over. Cardiac massage was vigorously recommenced as Hamish called for and was delivered strong drugs that would hopefully have the desired effect on the failing heart.

'Right, let's give them a minute to get in system—charge at 360.'

The defibrillator whirred into action as Cameron massaged the heart, giving the drugs a few vital seconds to hopefully reach their target before Hamish ordered everyone back and a shock was delivered.

The first of many.

On and on they worked, the smell of burning flesh filling the room as shock after shock was delivered—his tender age and the ongoing VF giving this patient the endless benefit of the doubt. But as time ticked on, the strain was telling on everyone. Hamish, was supremely controlled but grim with tension and everyone in the room wondered just how much longer they should continue.

'What did his father say *exactly*?' Hamish snapped the words at Cameron. 'I don't want to hear what you *think* he meant. How long was it before he got to him?' Endless stories had been delivered—the paramedics had been told by the father that they'd just finished milking when the accident had occurred and that the power had been turned off at source, and this had been confirmed when they'd arrived and they'd ensured the safety of the area before entering. But how long had it taken Vince to turn off the power and reach his son? Any further questioning of the paramedics was impossible as they had already been called away. When Amy had been sent in to find out she had been told that a safety switch had been tripped by his tearful father and now Cameron had come back with an equally conflicting story just to add to the confusion. 'No ones going to thank us if we get this guy back and he ends up spending the rest of his life in a nursing home! Now, I need to know,' Hamish snarled in exasperation. 'Where's Helen?'

'In an admin meeting,' Amy answered, chewing on her bottom lip as Hamish's eyes quickly scanned the room—no doubt wondering who to send next, two vertical lines appearing as he realised that the newest member of the team was probably the most appropriate... Apart from himself, Charlotte and the unfortunately absent Helen, it was a fairly junior team working this morning and the tension was mounting with each and every shock the defibrillator delivered. It was the dizziest, the most carefree amongst them who appeared the least affected—her hands utterly steady as she handed over drugs and kept an accurate log, each piece of information he demanded called back in a clear, unwavering voice. 'Charlotte, can you please go in there and get a decent history—preferably half an hour ago?'

Racing along the corridor to the interview room, Charlotte knocked and entered. As expected, Ronan's father was beside himself with anxiety, his rough, weather-beaten face wet with tears, his breathing coming so hard and fast he was on the verge of hyperventilating.

'I'm Charlotte, Charlotte Porter—I'm one of the nurses in with your son.'

'How is he?' Vince started, but Charlotte was already answering

'He's still very sick. We're still working very hard to get his heart started again. I need some more information from you.'

'I've already told everything I know. Why the hell are you all still asking me questions instead of dealing with my son?' Fear presented as anger but Charlotte ignored it, concentrating instead on staying on track. 'There are just a few things we need to clarify so we can do our best for Ronan. First, can you tell me your name?'

'Vince!' Exasperated as to what possible bearing it could have, he raised his palms to the air as he answered.

'Okay, Vince, I'm Charlotte.' Repeating her name, she gestured to the chair. 'Let's sit down while I ask you some questions. I know this is hard, but every detail is vital.' She watched as he clammed his jaws together, bit back a thousand questions and trusted that for now this stranger knew best. 'You'd just finished milking the cows—is that right?'

'I was loading the milk into the dairy truck. Ronan was fixing up a bit of equipment back in the milking shed…' She tried to picture it—her grandparents had had a dairy farm and it helped Charlotte envisage what he was saying as she prompted Vince to tell his tale.

'So how far from the shed were you?'

'A couple of hundred metres—if that,' Vince answered.

'And then what happened?'

'I heard a bang. I was up the ladder on the side of the truck, and as I turned around the milking shed went dark—I knew what had happened.'

'So then what did you do?' Charlotte pushed.

'I just ran over. I know I should have turned off the power—I just didn't stop, though—I knew the safety switch would have been tripped. Figured I had my gumboots on…' It had been a gamble, they both knew that, but panic, instinct to help his son had clearly taken over, regardless of the consequences to himself. 'I started CPR straight away. I've told the doctor this and that nurse. I did an instructor's course for first aid last year…'

'Who turned the power off?' Charlotte asked. 'It was off when the paramedics arrived.'

'The truck driver—he was running behind to help and I knew I'd already taken a risk—I didn't want him doing it. I told him to go…'

She'd got the history they so badly needed and Charlotte didn't wait for the rest, just headed for the door with one final question.

'How long from the ladder to Ronan?'

'A minute, if that.' Vince sobbed. 'Charlotte, you have to help him—please, tell the doctors that they mustn't give up!'

She paused for just a fraction of a second to give him one promise. 'Vince, no one will stop in there without talking to you first.'

'A minute!' Running into Resus Charlotte delivered the vital information and Hamish gave a grateful nod. 'He was down for no more than a minute—and the dad's recently done a first-aid course.'

As Hamish called for yet more drugs, as the defibrillator was recharged and the vigorous resuscitation continued, Charlotte elaborated on what Vince had told her but Hamish was barely listening, satisfied now it was more than appropriate to continue.

'If we have to stop, I've told the father someone will go in and talk to him first,' Charlotte told Hamish, watching him for a reaction. As painful as it was for relatives to see their loved ones being worked on, sometimes it was appropriate to offer, for people to see and understand that despite the best of efforts there was nothing that could be done, and she was sure that Vince would want to be the one to make the call.

'Sure.' Hamish gave a brief nod. 'Everyone back!'

Cameron was just about to resume compressions again when Hamish halted him. A flicker of a heartbeat had appeared on the screen, only instead of elation there was still a sense of trepidation as Hamish felt first the patient's carotid artery and then moved his hand to his wrist. 'We've got a radial pulse—have we got a blood pressure?'

'Sixty,' Charlotte called, holding her breath as the monitor showed that the weak, thready pulse that had first flickered had been replaced now by strong regular bleeps, helped along by the drugs Hamish was delivering into his vein.

'We've got him,' Hamish said, staring at his team with a quiet nod of appreciation for their efforts. 'At least for the moment. Does anyone know if ICU has a bed?'

'It's full,' the anaesthetist answered, then glanced down at his trilling pager and used irony to soften the fact that someone had just lost their fight for life on ICU. 'Scrap what I said. It would seem that a bed just came up—it must be this guy's lucky day!'

Heading to the interview room with Hamish to inform Vince about what was happening, even if Ronan's prognosis was extremely guarded it was still way better than had been hoped for.

'I'm going to paint it pretty black for him.' Hamish caught her arm just before they reached the door. 'If it sounds as if I'm being harsh, then that's how I intend it be.'

'Sure!' Charlotte replied easily.

'Sure?' He frowned down at her glib response, surprised at how unperturbed she appeared at the prospect of speaking to Vince. Yes, she was experienced, but so was he, and even after all this time, breaking bad news was never pleasant. But Charlotte didn't notice his frown, wasn't even looking back at him. Instead, she stared at her arm, stared at each freckle and hair, stared at the pale flesh that should surely show the burn his fingers had made—not that he had grabbed her, his fingers had barely made contact...

But it had been their first touch.

They'd lived together for four days, had shared meals, conversations and passed Bailey between them and yet, Charlotte realised, it was the first time they'd actually touched.

'This could be really difficult,' Hamish elaborated. 'I just want to make sure we're on the same page.'

'In all probability his son's going to die…' Tearing her eyes from her arm, Charlotte met his stare as she responded. 'Or worse, he's going to be brain damaged—so, no, don't fret. I'm not going to go in there waving streamers and telling him it's time to crack open the champagne.'

'Good.' Hamish nodded and took a deep breath. 'Let's do it.'

'What's happening?' Pacing the tiny interview room like a caged animal, Vince stopped and hurled the question the second they entered. 'Charlotte—what's happening?'

'Sit down, Vince.' Her voice was incredibly firm, directing this huge, agitated man to a chair, and Hamish noted that with just three little words she had paved the difficult way for him. By not jumping in, by not hurriedly telling him that they'd managed to get Ronan's heart beating again, Vince was actually expecting to hear that his son had or—because of Charlotte's promise—was about to die. His ruddy face rested in his rough hands as he braced himself for the words no parent ever wanted to hear.

'Ronan is very ill.' Sitting in the chair opposite him, Hamish watched as his words sank in, as the wail of grief that had surely been building was stifled. 'It took a very long time to get his heart beating on its own again.'

'But it is?' Vince's voice was a croak.

'Yes.' Hamish nodded. 'Right now he's intubated and we're trying to stabilise him enough to move him to Intensive Care, but I have to warn you…'

'He might have brain damage?'

'That's one of our main concerns,' Hamish responded.

'I worked on him straight away, Doc. I was telling Charlotte here that I'd done the instructor's course for first aid.' Pleading eyes jerked to Charlotte. 'I know how to do CPR.'

'You did an amazing job,' Charlotte responded, and it was appropriate that she did so. Bonds were quickly established in the most dire of circumstances and the fleeting interview had clearly forged these. Hamish didn't intervene, realising that, for whatever reason, Vince clearly needed to hear Charlotte's take on things. 'There was absolutely nothing more you could have done for your son—you've given him the best possible chance in the most dire of circumstances. However, the resuscitation was extremely prolonged and as Dr Adams said, brain damage is a very real possibility.'

'What's the other major concern the doctor was talking about?' Vince still stared at Charlotte, but this yorker was one Hamish was ready to bat and taking a deep breath he was about to face it, only Charlotte was already there, answering Vince's most difficult question with the most direct of answers.

'That he may well die.' Her voice was clear as she delivered brutal words that even the most experienced, most senior of staff struggled with. Suddenly Hamish was back in the intensive care unit, sitting in a room so similar to this one, clinging to the words Ned, his friend and colleague, had gently delivered.

'Hold her hand and talk to her, Hamish.'

'Can she hear me?'

'I hope so.'

'Is there any chance…?'

'Of course there's a chance.' After the longest of pauses, Ned had nodded. *'Where there's life there's hope, Hamish.'*

God, how he'd clung to that—clung to the old adage as he'd clung to Emma's pale hand, willing her to live with kisses, words and tears, because if a neurosurgeon had said there was hope, then surely he'd meant it.

But there had been no *hope.*

The second her CT scan had appeared on the screen, Ned would have known that, known that the only thing keeping this beautiful vital woman breathing had been the machine pushing air into her lungs—that behind her still perfect features her brain had been putty. How Hamish had wanted to ram all his anger at Ned when the truth had hit—payback for those wretched, tortured hours where he'd dared to believe that Emma might come back to him, that Bailey might grow up with a mother, and all because it had seemed better at the time than telling him the stark truth.

Whether he realised it or not, Vince was a lucky man.

'Is there any hope?'

For a full minute the room had been silent, only it hadn't been uncomfortable, the two men lost in their thoughts as Charlotte had patiently sat. It was Vince who had, in his own time, broken it.

'We'll know more soon,' Hamish answered carefully. Ronan, even in this most fragile state, had more hope than Emma had ever had, but realistically his heart could stop again at any time. 'We haven't given up on him by any means.'

'Can I see him?'

'Of course,' Hamish said gently, standing up to take Vince to see his son. 'If we ask you to step aside…'

'I won't get in the way, Doctor—I know he needs you lot more than me right now.'

And then Hamish did the strangest thing—something he'd never done, even before Emma's death had frozen him on the inside. As they reached Ronan, Hamish reached out and gripped the other man's arm to support him as he surveyed the shell of his son, offered him a little piece of himself that wasn't just a doctor. 'I'm so sorry for all you're going through.'

'Thanks.' Vince gulped. 'That means a lot.'

'As I've said, these wounds are just the tip of the iceberg,' Hamish explained to the gathered group of doctors and nurses, pointing to the two black burns on Vince's feet. 'The electricity entered his body here.' Hamish held up a limp hand. 'And his feet are where the electricity exited the body.' Leaning under the trolley, he pulled out Ronan's gumboots and showed them to the gathered crowd—the two holes clearly visible. 'If it can do this to boots, then you can imagine the damage it's wreaked inside to nerves, veins and arteries on its journey. Did you want to join us?' Hamish asked as Charlotte popped her head around the door and interrupted his impromptu lecture.

'ICU just called—they're ready for Ronan.'

'Fine…' Hamish nodded as the crowd dispersed, stepping back as she ran a final set of obs on Ronan, and for the second time his arm caught Charlotte's—waiting till she was finished with the patient before discreetly drawing her aside.

'I think you make a very good teacher!'

'Thanks but, no, thanks!' Hamish shook his head and smiled, but it faded, his voice more serious now. 'Are you okay?'

'Fine,' Charlotte answered. 'Well, dying for my coffee-break but I guess that will have to wait till I've taken him up and then cleared up the mess.'

'You were very good with his father.'

'Thanks.'

'And you're okay with everything that happened this morning?' There was just a smudge of a frown on her face, as if she was curious as to why he'd even be checking. 'I mean, it's been a pretty intense morning.'

'That's Emergency for you.' Charlotte shrugged. 'Honestly, Hamish, I'm fine. Just doing my job like the rest of us.'

Only she wasn't like the rest of them, Hamish thought as she breezed along the corridor, grabbing a blanket from the linen trolley and stopping for a quick chat and giggle with Mike the porter—watching with more than slight bemusement as the old boy wiggled his hips at a delighted Charlotte and did a strange little dance.

He couldn't fault a single thing she'd done that morning—she'd been efficient and capable in resuscitation, incredibly intuitive and helpful in dealing with relatives, all the staff liked her, every patient she came in contact with seemed to adore her, and yet… Hamish flicked through his mental thesaurus, trying to find the word he was looking for that summed up the vague uneasiness she generated in him at times.

Detached—that was the best he could come up with. Despite her warm demeanour, despite her engaging smile, there was this cool detachment to Charlotte that didn't add up. The more he thought about it, nothing seemed to upset her, nothing seemed to really faze her, nothing really seemed to bother Charlotte at all. In fact, sometimes it was as if…

He didn't like the conclusion he was inching towards to, felt guilty almost for even thinking it, given the way she was at home and with Bailey and her impressive skills at work… But still the nagging voice wouldn't go away.

Sometimes it was if Charlotte had pushed her true emotions about *everything* so far down that she didn't feel them at all.

Maybe it *was* Ronan's lucky day! Transferring him from Accident and Emergency's equipment to that of ICU's, Charlotte watched in awe as the anaesthetist rolled his pen along Ronan's arm and Ronan actually pulled his hand away.

'Withdrawal to pain. Boy, this job never ceases to amaze me. I was about to tell your boss he was wasting everyone's time. Looks like we might just have a happy ending here,' the anaesthetist said.

Wandering parched back down the corridor and grabbing a bottle of diet cola from the machine, she saw the sign for the paediatric ward and Charlotte decided she had more than earned a break. She was so glad she did when little Andy's face lit up in delight at his most welcome visitor, delighted to see him playing a board game with another little boy who was sitting on his bed.

'Are you *still* here?' Feigning surprise, she gave him wide-eyed look.

'I'm staying in for a while!' Andy nodded proudly. 'They're giving me lots of treatment for my skin and they've put me on this disgusting diet—I have to go under the sun lamps and mum's getting my new glasses this afternoon—this is Blake,' he added without pausing for a single breath, 'he's got really bad eczema and it's all infected!'

'Bad luck, Blake,' Charlotte gave a sympathetic smile. 'I just popped in to say hi. I really can't stop, but I'll come and see you again as soon as I can.'

'Promise?' Andy checked.

'I promise.'

It was a smiling Charlotte that walked back into Emergency, only to be greeted by a rather strained-looking Cameron. 'I'm supposed to have a word with you,' he said as she headed back to clear up Resus.

'Supposed to?' Charlotte checked.

'Boss's orders.' Cameron let out a long sigh. 'I really messed it up back there. Hamish said I should talk with some of the more experienced nursing staff—someone who was used to dealing with upset relatives. He suggested you, given how you'd spoken to the father as well and got him to make sense. Vince was just all over the place. I couldn't make head or tail of what he was saying. I'm going cold thinking that they might have stopped the resuscitation just—'

'They wouldn't have,' Charlotte said kindly. 'Just knowing the facts made it a lot easier to continue.'

'Coffee-break, Charlotte,' Helen called briskly as Charlotte entered the swing doors, every last shred of the morning's chaos jut a memory now, the ever-efficient Helen wasting no time in getting the resuscitation area back into shape for the next visitor.

'Do you want to talk now?' Charlotte offered. 'We could go to the interview room—it's a bit more private than the staffroom.'

'Don't you need a coffee?'

'Caffeine's caffeine.' Charlotte grinned, holding up her half-drunk bottle of cola. 'Whatever way it's delivered. Come on.'

'I just didn't know how to calm him down,' Cameron explained, after telling his side of the story and sounding more than a touch embarrassed. 'Vince kept asking me how his son was doing, what was happening, if he'd done the right thing—only I couldn't get him to explain *exactly* what he'd done, and it just seemed tactless to ignore his questions when he was so desperate for information.'

'I find the best way is to explain the urgency of the situation,' Charlotte offered. 'That for now, to help their relative, answers will just have to wait—and even if you do appear tactless at the time, you can always go back and explain why afterwards. If they start to digress, just tell the family or whoever that for the moment you need some very direct answers to some very specific questions and don't be afraid to ask them.'

'It's hard, though,' Cameron sighed. 'How long have you been doing this?'

'I've been in Emergency for six years,' Charlotte smiled, 'and, honestly, talking to relatives does get easier. You should go and sit in as much as you can when someone else is trying to get a rapid history or break difficult news. Not only will you pick up some tips, you'll see for yourself ways *not* to go about it.'

'So how old does that make you?' Cameron asked as they stood up to go.

'Twenty-eight,' Charlotte groaned. 'Inching ever closer to the big three-oh!'

'Thanks for your help.' Cameron grinned. 'I owe you a drink.'

'You do,' Charlotte responded.

'How about Saturday?'

Hamish walking past at that very moment shouldn't have mattered a jot—only somehow it did. And Cameron's invitation had very little to do with her flushing and unbecoming shade of purple.

'Sorry.' Cameron grimaced. 'I didn't realise he was around.'

'Who?'

'Hamish,' Cameron answered—and even if it was the correct answer, Charlotte had no idea how it should be the obvious one. 'I heard you two were sharing a house—I guess I should have checked you were just housemates before asking you out!'

'We are,' Charlotte replied. 'There's absolutely nothing going on between us…'

'You're sure about that?'

'Positive.' Charlotte nodded.

'So—there isn't a problem if I pick you up on Saturday.'

'Actually, there is one!' In a fabulous impersonation of Cassie, Charlotte beat her blush and shook her head. 'I've already got plans.'

She did have plans!

A serious lie-in, a few hours' shopping and then some serious dancing!

Despite the rather ominous start, her first week at Adams farm had turned out well. Her day spent with Bailey had been invaluable: getting to know the little boy in his own surroundings had been the right move and when Hamish had knocked on her door at two in the morning with a grizzling Bailey, apologising that he had to go into work, Bailey hadn't kicked up a fuss when his father had left—in fact by the time the first weekend came around Charlotte felt as if she had been there for months and Hamish was wondering when this woman ever slept!

'What have you been doing?'

'Getting the stables ready,' Charlotte beamed, stomping into the kitchen and pulling open the pantry door at seven-thirty on Saturday morning dressed in nothing more than a flimsy white cotton nightdress and a pair of gumboots—as a rather un-together Hamish worked his way through a mug of coffee. 'They arrive next Saturday—I might not get a chance during the week. I was just checking for any loose nails and putting down some straw. We're out of bread.'

'I think there's some in the freezer.'

'There isn't.' It only took a quick glance to answer him—no rummaging at the back or pulling out of food had been necessary to check that, apart from ice cubes and a rather tragic-looking apple pie, it was empty.

'If we leave in the next half-hour it shouldn't be too busy,'

'What shouldn't?'

'The supermarket. We need to go shopping.'

'Shopping?'

She smiled at his bemused frown. 'Don't tell me— Elsie did it for you.'

'I shop.'

'At the local take-away or garage! Hamish, there's *no* food in the house.'

'I'll get some groceries in tomorrow.'

'And what will we eat tonight?'

'I'm sure there's a can of beans at the back of the cupboard.'

'Boring!'

'I'll grate some cheese on them.' Hamish gave a tight smile. 'Anyway, what does it matter to you? You're going out.'

'No, I'm not.'

'With Cameron,' Hamish said patiently. 'I heard him asking you out—remember?'

It was the first time they'd raised the uncomfortable subject—the first time that living and working together, just as Hamish had predicted it would, had actually raised its head.

'So you just assumed I said yes.' Charlotte gave a

very knowing smile as Hamish had the decency to colour up a touch.

'I just thought…'

'Oh, I know what you thought, a good-looking doctor asks little nursy out on a Saturday night—so, of course, she's going!' It was Charlotte colouring up a touch now, the teasing note in her voice disappearing. 'He knows that we're sharing a house. I didn't tell anyone,' Charlotte added hurriedly. 'I've no idea how he could know.'

'You would have filled in a change of address form.' Hamish said, and Charlotte nodded glumly.

'Adams Farm?' Hamish checked, and it was followed by another glum nod. 'And I assume that you gave your new phone number for the emergency staff book…I'm called in so often that most of the senior staff know it off by heart. It was always going to get out, Charlotte.'

'I just never thought it would be so soon.'

'You're driving my Jeep.'

'I'm sorry.'

'Don't be—I knew it would happen. There's no chance of a private life when you work in a hospital.' He gave a tight shrug. 'Maybe you should have said yes to Cameron, for no other reason than to stop the impending marriage in its tracks.'

'Marriage?' She gave him a startled look, caught his eye in horror, and Hamish grinned back as he spoke— for the first time he felt as if he was actually looking her, glimpsing the real Charlotte. 'Well, this time next week that's what they'll all be saying…' But even before he had finished speaking the moment was gone as she threw her head back and laughed, and he realised he had been mistaken.

'Why on earth would we worry about a little bit of paper when we can settle for a torrid affair—or even shopping?'

'I *hate* shopping!'

'Because you've never been with an expert.' Charlotte rummaged in her bag and pulled out a diary, clicking on her ballpoint and smiling at him. 'I suppose I could just buy my stuff and label it, as I did when I lived in the youth hostel, or I could hazard a guess as to what you and Bailey like and take pot luck. Well?'

'Well, what?'

'Look, if you really don't want to hit the supermarket, I'll write a list. Tell me what you like, what Bailey likes—oh, his nappies are getting low and we're running out of washing powder. Write down what type you use—'

'Okay, okay.'

'Do you need any toiletries—what brand?'

'I get the message, Charlotte.'

'What message?'

'We'll all go. I just need to change Bailey's nappy first.'

'Brilliant.' Charlotte beamed, rummaging in that blessed bag and pulling out her car keys. 'I'll drive!'

On cue, Bailey waddled in and didn't go directly to his dad, instead aiming straight for Charlotte. As she bent over to pick him up it was impossible not to notice the soft flesh of her breasts threatening to spill out of her flimsy nightdress.

'Er, Charlotte…' He stared at her, Bailey balanced

on one hip, her face flushed from the exertion of unloading the horses, without a scrap of make-up, dark curls tied up in knots from the absence of a brushing, still in that nighty and gumboots, and he'd never seen her more beautiful. It was impossible not to smile, impossible not to adore her and impossible not to wonder if she were wearing any panties! 'Shouldn't you get dressed first?'

She stared down, aghast. 'Heavens, yes!' Plonking Bailey down, she ran to the stairs as she called out to him over her shoulder. 'I'd have gone, you know—if you hadn't told me I'd be walking around the supermarket…'

Her voice faded as she climbed the stairs, but instead of changing Bailey's nappy, instead of trying to locate his wallet or checking the pantry for what was needed—everything—Hamish just stood there…

'Dar-dot!' Bailey stared at his dad, as if reading his mind. 'Want Dar-dot.'

'I know the feeling, buddy,' Hamish said under his breath, then, picking up his son, he stared at the muddy footprints her gumboots had left the length of the hallway—like some decadent yellow brick road that he was tempted to follow. Her dog and cat sat forlornly at the bottom of the steps, waiting for her to come down, and at that moment both he and Bailey could have joined them.

She'd spun into his world on her own self-fuelled tornado, filled his empty home with animals, laughter and gentle bullying—it was eight o'clock on a Saturday morning and here they were, heading for the shops. The spare room was painted, Bailey far happier than he ever had been, and as for Hamish…

His stomach tightened with lust and something else which at the moment he couldn't define, something he hadn't felt in a long time.

His good mood soon evaporated. For Hamish there was nothing attractive about Saturday morning at a supermarket—early they might be, but every family in town had had the same idea and it took for ever to find a parking spot, then, attempting to pull out a trolley he discovered that since last he'd done this, he now needed a coin—which did nothing to add to his distracted and slightly testy mood. But Charlotte was in her element, loading Bailey into his little throne and steering her trolley like a woman on a mission.

'What are you doing?' Hamish snapped, as she replaced the loaf of bread he had picked up and replaced it with two of a different brand.

'Buy one, get one free!' Rummaging in her bag, she pulled out a huge silver bulldog clip holding together bundles of paper. 'Coupons!'

'*You* cut out shopping coupons!'

'Of course I do! We're not all on a consultant's salary.'

'This is bad enough, Charlotte, without having to…' He peered through the mountain of coupons she had diligently clipped. 'We'll be here for ever.'

'So relax and enjoy it!'

Easier said than done.

'Hamish!' Well groomed, well dressed and, well, just a little pushy, one of the mums from crèche caught up with him as he was wrestling a huge box of nappies from the top shelf, as opposed to the small pack he usually purchased, while Charlotte checked out the gum gel. 'No luck with the potty training, then?'

'None,' Hamish said grimly. 'How did it go with Felicity?'

'Great. She's actually dry through the night now. Oh, hello!' Despite her smile, there was defiantly a frown on her face and a rather awkward moment ensued as Charlotte came over, her hands full of lotions and potions, completely unable to make a choice.

'This is Charlotte.' Hamish started to introduce, then came another awkward moment when he realised he didn't actually know Felicity's mother's name. 'She lives with me.'

'Oh!'

'Well sort of…' Hamish offered, wishing he'd never agreed to come shopping.

'I'm the live-in babysitter.' Charlotte gave a warm smile. 'And you are…?'

'Lucy!' The frown that looked as if it had been tattooed on faded just a touch. 'So you two aren't…'

'Goodness, no.' Charlotte laughed as the two vertical lines evaporated completely. 'He's way too miserable for me.'

'You know, I bought Felicity a lovely potty. When she goes it plays a little song—of course she's past that now, she's sitting on the toilet.'

'Fantastic!' Hamish attempted.

'You're welcome to borrow it when you want to have another try with Bailey. Catch me at crèche drop-off one morning if you want it and you can call around and pick it up.'

'Sure.' Once she'd gone, Hamish gave a miserable sigh. 'Maybe I *should* just buy the little pack after all and *really* give this potty training a go.'

Still, after that, shopping was surprisingly easy—Charlotte made it surprisingly easy. Whipping out a little carton of apple juice from that oversized handbag when Bailey started grizzling, piling the trolley with food, essentials and an awful lot of goodies as she chattered on incessantly. Even the formidable queue was made bearable when finally he followed her lead.

She was leafing through magazines, brazenly reading anything that caught her interest, then, without even a hint of blush, putting them back and moving on to the next one as the checkout operator gave her a baleful look.

'You can't just read them and not buy them!'

'If more aisles were open, I wouldn't need to read their magazines.' Charlotte shrugged. 'Ooh, I think I *will* buy this one—apparently my finances are going to improve and I'm going to fall head over heels in love…' Screwing up her nose, she suddenly put it back. 'It says to watch my health. What does yours say?' Charlotte asked, inching the trolley along and starting to unload, smiling as he actually picked up a glossy and thumbed his way through it.

'That if I'm not careful I'm going to be completely corrupted—Bailey, too…' Hamish gave an apologetic nod to the now extremely irritated checkout operator as his son reached over and clamped his hand over a bar of chocolate. 'No, Bailey!'

'Oh, he's been so good, just let him have it,' Charlotte said, peeling off the wrapper and handing it to the checkout assistant, dazzling her with her smile as she unloaded their groaning trolley. 'How are you?' Charlotte beamed before the assistant even had a chance to deliver the weary question of her own. 'Worn out, I'll bet, with these queues and everyone moaning about delays. Why on earth don't they open more checkouts and make things a touch easier for you?'

And somehow she did it again. The miserable, irritable checkout operator was now gratefully taking the opportunity to moan about management and customers and people who thought their children could help themselves to whatever they wanted at the checkout.

'Not like you, of course…' She gave the three of them a fond smile as she tore off the receipt. 'At least you remembered to hand over the wrapper. You make a lovely family.'

'Thanks,' Charlotte said, steering the trolley towards the café, ignoring Hamish's sudden dark mood. 'Ooh, smell that bacon.'

'Let's just get home.'

'Surely we can have just a quick coffee!'

Which for Charlotte meant the full breakfast! Sitting down with her laden tray in the cosy café, she ignored Hamish's baleful look.

'You shouldn't have said that,' Hamish said when finally she was organised and tucking into a mountain of bacon, eggs and beans. Bailey was happily chomping on a large muffin.

'Said what?' Charlotte smiled. 'Are you sure you don't want some breakfast?'

'That we were a family.'

'Oh, for goodness' sake!' Tearing open a roll, she ignored the shake of his head and crammed it with bacon and handed it to him. When still he shook his head, she popped it on a side plate and left it on the table in front of him. 'And you did so well with Lucy—you practically told her I was your new lover.'

'Well, I'll know better next time,' Hamish snapped. 'But you let that woman think we were actually a family…'

'She was just making conversation, for goodness' sake. What was I supposed to say to the poor woman? "Well, actually, he was widowed last year, the little guy hasn't got a mum—oh, and while we're on the subject my mum actually just sold the family home and flew off with her latest lover to Queensland, technically leaving me and all my pets homeless…"'

'Oh, Helen! Over here!' Charlotte stood up and waved as Hamish tried to sink lower in his seat as their strange living arrangement was suddenly outed again.

'You said you were discreet!' Hamish hissed. 'What the hell did you have to call her over for?'

'Why wouldn't I?' Charlotte blinked as Helen gave a delighted wave and made her way over. 'Everyone knows anyway!'

'But we look like…' He stared around the café, at all the tables filled with couples and toddlers and groaning trolleys, but Charlotte missed his point.

'We're not snogging.' She giggled. 'We're not sitting

holding hands across the table while I feed you with my fork. We are allowed to eat, you know, and shop. Relax, would you?'

He had no intention of relaxing!

None at all, though when Helen barely turned a hair, just gave a vague 'hi' to him then proceeded to chat to Charlotte about a new shoe purchase, he wasn't left with much choice but to give in, give up his bad mood and drink his coffee.

'I took your advice and got them, Charlotte…' Helen rummaged in the carrier bag. 'You like my new shoes, Hamish?'

He was about to give a polite nod and smile when Helen pulled out a pair of brown flats, or whatever shoes sixty-year-old women wore, but as Helen pulled out a pair of very high, very red stilettos, somehow he knew he mustn't catch Charlotte's eyes, knew that if he did, he'd start laughing.

'They're…nice.'

'Gorgeous.' Charlotte beamed. And Hamish decided that the world had gone mad!

And finally he did relax, taking the roll and biting in to it, chatting to Bailey yet glancing over every now and then as Charlotte oohed and ahhed with Helen.

Trying and failing to make her out.

Today was the first time she'd even so much as indicated that her own life was less than perfect, the first time he'd even glimpsed at what went on behind that happy, scattered thought process, and Hamish, finally admitted to himself that he wanted to hear more…*really* wanted to get know the real Charlotte.

And later, when the groceries had long been put away and his whole day had been spent avoiding thinking, he walked into the family room to see her curled up, reading on the sofa, idly eating an apple and wearing glasses he'd never seen her in before. Weak in the knees with longing, finally he could avoid it no more, condensed his thoughts just a touch further...

He really wanted her...

'Where's Bailey?' Smiling quizzically at him just standing there, Charlotte looked up from her book.

'Teasing the cat!' Hamish gave a tight smile, feeling like a lech for being caught staring, feeling like an idiot just standing there, but his mind was working overtime, wondering if he could ring Bel and ask her to babysit, then wondering what the hell he would do then! He hadn't asked a woman out in over a decade! And if he did ask her and she said no, how awkward would that make things? And if he did ask her and she said yes...

'What time is it?'

'Six.' Hamish stared down at his watch. 'Charlotte, I was just thinking—'

'Six!' Horrified, she jumped up. 'Oh, God, I got lost. I've been reading for hours! I'm going to be late! Sorry...' Spinning out the room, she paused momentarily. 'What were you thinking?'

'Nothing.' Hamish shook his head. 'You'd better get on.'

Pulling out his laptop, sitting on the sofa, he was incredibly grateful to have been saved from his moment of madness when Bailey climbed up beside him.

'Mum,' he said, pointing to the screensaver and cuddling in.

'That's right,' Hamish said, staring at the three of them, remembering Belinda taking the photo, babysitting for the very first time as they'd headed out to the consultants' ball. Bailey a tiny smudge of pink peeking out of his bunny rug, himself uncomfortable in a tux and Emma stunning in an elegant black dress, her blonde hair swept up in a roll… Hamish was knocked out of his reverie when Charlotte appeared again.

'Right, I'm off—how do I look?'

Like a rather gorgeous courtesan, actually!

He didn't say that, of course, but as Charlotte teetered into the family room all sparkly and dressed up for her night on the town, never had Hamish felt more boring and staid or grateful for the very near miss that had, unbeknownst to Charlotte, just taken place.

They could never, *ever* have worked—he'd been an absolute fool to even entertain it. Staring up at her, he even managed a very dry smile—just imagine taking *that* as his date to the upcoming consultants' ball!

Apart from lethal stilettos she was wearing a sapphire-blue satin skirt, with layers and layers of ruffles, her pert bosom on show in a very revealing top and about a gallon of eyeliner and red lipstick. Add to that spectacularly teased hair with a massive flower threaded into it, and for a second he wondered if she wasn't teetering on the edge of a manic phase!

'Very nice,' Hamish managed, watching wide-eyed and tempted to cover Bailey's as she picked up her skirt and did a strange little dance for him. But luckily her lift arrived, a car tooting in the driveway, and with a quick goodnight Charlotte kicked up her heels and ran.

'Pretty!' Bailey clapped when the door slammed and their Saturday night's entertainment was over. 'Where's Dar-dot?'

'You're too young to know,' Hamish quipped, then shook his head. 'And I'm definitely too old!'

CHAPTER FIVE

'You must be getting excited about your animals arriving!' Helen stretched her swollen legs out in front of her as she tapped away on the computer and tried to smother a yawn—a stint of night duty the last thing she'd wanted or needed. But at least the place was quiet and the day staff were starting to arrive.

'I can't wait!' Charlotte nodded, a touch rushed this morning, given Hamish had been called in at six and she'd had to take Bailey to child care. 'What are you doing?'

'Trying to get the results of for some bloods for the patient in four—Hamish wants them before he rings Cardiology. The man's ECG is still showing a normal reading, but Hamish is sure he's had had a heart attack. The lab says they've sent them but the computer still says pending. I hate these things.' she moaned. 'Now it's frozen on me. Why can't they just ring down the results like they used to?'

'Here,' Charlotte said, plonking down her bag and pulling up a chair beside the technically challenged Helen. 'I'll have a go.'

'Have you got those results yet, Helen?' Irritated and gorgeous, Hamish marched into the nurses' station as Charlotte tried to see what Helen had been doing.

'They're just coming,' Charlotte answered, then carried on talking to Helen. 'The journey will be tough on Scottie…'

'He's the old pony?' Helen checked.

'That's the one.' Charlotte nodded. 'Here, we're up.'

'But it still says pending,' Helen sighed. 'Oh, I'll ring the lab again.'

'You have to hit the "refresh" button, Helen.' Charlotte giggled. 'If you want to update the results, you have to press "refresh." I told you that.'

'So you did. We've got them, Hamish.'

'Right…' Peering at the screen, Hamish gave a brisk nod. 'He's had an infarct—I'll get on to Cardiology.'

'He's just so-o-o cute,' Charlotte said dreamily, as Hamish did a double-take while he picked up the phone. 'Scottie, not you.' She winked. The fact they were sharing a house was general knowledge now, and at work at least Charlotte was still incredibly discreet, but given that apart from them the nurses' station was empty and Helen was a good friend of Hamish's, in front of her they chatted more easily. 'You know, Bailey could have a little ride on him. He's such a gentle old thing.'

'Bailey's not to go near him,' Hamish said sternly.

'But Scottie wouldn't harm a fly.'

'I do not want my son anywhere near the stables,' Hamish barked, then, turning his back, he spoke to the cardiology reg.

'Leave it, Charlotte.' Helen was practically doing semaphore signals across the nurses' station in an effort to quiet her. 'I'll talk to you in a minute.'

'It would be good for him,' Charlotte still insisted, as Hamish put down the phone.

'I decide what's good for my son,' Hamish retorted, stalking off and calling over his shoulder, 'You're the live-in help—remember that. You follow *my* rules.'

'Sourpuss!' Charlotte muttered, but only when he was safely out of earshot.

'With good reason on this occasion.' Helen took a deep breath then spoke in a low whisper. 'His wife died as a result of a riding accident—she fell off and was trampled, right there in front of him. He was making up a bottle for Bailey in the kitchen and he saw it all.'

'Oh.'

And Helen waited, waited for Charlotte to colour up and give a mortified moan, as anyone would. 'You can say sorry to him later,' she added kindly, 'when he's calmed down a touch!'

'Me? Say sorry! Did you hear how rude he just was?' Charlotte spluttered, giving Helen a queer look and logging out of the blood results. Despite the presence of her boss, she logged onto her emails and quickly checked out her free tarot reading for the day before they headed over to check the drugs. 'It's awful that he's lost his wife and that Bailey's lost his mother, it truly is, but all I can say is that it's just as well Emma didn't die in motor vehicle accident or I'd *still* be pushing Bailey in his stroller all the way to day care!'

* * *

Even if they were both still smarting, when her friend arrived at the crack of dawn with her beloved animals and a mountain of boxes, despite himself Hamish did pull on some jeans and boots and head out to help Charlotte unload.

'Poor Scottie, he's just exhausted from his journey… What he needs is a good rest and a nice feed.'

What Scottie needs is a bullet, Hamish thought, staring in astonishment as the oldest horse, or rather pony, he had every seen limped his way down the ramp—woefully underweight, his hips were protruding and Hamish wondered how his think shaky legs managed to hold him up. His hooves were encased in leather bootees, thanks to a prolonged bout of laminitis, and he was neighing in terror as Charlotte urged the old boy on. No, he wasn't just old, Hamish decided. On closer inspection this was the Father Time of the horsy world—to call Scottie a pony was almost a sin itself. Quite simply, Scottie was ancient.

'Poor old boy,' said Trevor, Charlotte's friend, who had driven two hours out of his way just for her, and was now helping her to get him in the stable. Hamish, tentatively at first, found himself joining in. 'I'll go and check on Fitz and unload the last of your boxes. You stay with Scottie. He'll soon settle now he's got you.'

'Oh, I hope so.' For once Charlotte actually looked upset, hugging Scottie's neck and shushing him to calm down. 'Maybe the journey was too much for him.'

'Well, you couldn't just leave him where he was,' Trevor pointed out, rolling his eyes at Hamish as the two men walked out of the stable. He added, in a voice that wasn't meant for Charlotte's ears, 'Thanks to her bloody mother.'

Fitz was fine, his head peering out of the stable door, sniffing at the new air and nudging Trevor for a treat when he passed.

'I'm sure Charlotte's got plenty waiting for you!' Trevor said.

'Fancy a cuppa?' Hamish offered as they dumped her boxes in the corner of the family room—and not only because it was the polite thing to do. He was rather hoping Trevor might elaborate on what he'd said earlier.

'That'd be great—then I'd better head off.'

'There's no rush,' Hamish said. 'Stay for some breakfast?'

'Thanks anyway, but I'd really better make a move. I think the wife's got a few jobs line up for me today.'

'Whereabouts are you picking up the other horses from?' Hamish watched as Trevor frowned then laughed.

'Oh, that's what I told Charlotte—she'll be wanting to pay me otherwise. Always giving out favours, that one, but she doesn't know how to take them herself.'

'Sounds as if Charlotte's taken a lot on…' Hamish's throat went dry as he fished a little further. 'What with her mother leaving so quickly and everything.'

'Josie?' Trevor rolled his eyes—eggs and bacon clearly not required to get him talking! 'Blooming minx!' Hamish gave a noncommittal smile and spooned some sugar he didn't take into his brew. 'You know, since her marriage broke up it's been one fancy man after another. Still, I was just saying to the wife that this one should keep her quiet for a while—given that he comes with all the trimmings.' He registered Hamish's frown. 'You know, the fancy car, the boat…' He tapped his fingers as he worked through the list. 'You'd think they'd see through her; though…' Trevor leant over the table '…and I would never say it to the missus, of course, but I can see how Josie wraps them around her little finger—I mean, she's a good-looking woman, and always laughing and having fun. Not that she'd even look at old goat like me—unless she needed something!'

'He seems to be settling.' Trevor abruptly stopped talking as Charlotte came into the kitchen. 'Thank you so much, Trevor, you've no idea how grateful I am for your help. Now, how much do I owe you?'

'Nothing,' Trevor said, shaking his head as she pulled out her purse. 'I already told you I was coming down this way.'

'You've been over every day, feeding them.'

'It's no big deal!'

'Let me give you the petrol money at least,' Charlotte insisted, but Trevor was having none of it, quickly changing the subject.

'I was looking through the windows of your house when I picked up the boys—it looks as if there's a lot of work to be done there before the new owners move in on Monday. Do you need a hand? I can come and help with some of the heavy stuff.'

'Nope—it's all under control. I'm off Thursday and Friday. I've got a charity shop coming first to take their pick of what's left and I've rented the biggest skip in the world, and if I work like a maniac, by five o'clock Friday I'll be handing the keys to the real-estate agent.'

'What about cleaning the place?'

'I've got it all under control—I'm hiring a cleaner for a few hours on the Friday.'

'You're not hiring anyone,' Trevor scolded. 'I'll be there to help on Thursday and the wife will be there seven o'clock Friday morning to help with the cleaning—it's all been arranged, so no arguments!'

Scottie did seem to settle in quickly—it was Bailey who was fretful. Sensing the activity outside all morning, he grizzled to get out there, pointing his finger and dancing on the spot as Hamish refused to understand what it was he was asking to do. Even dancing along with him to his favourite video barely raised a smile.

'What are you two doing, cooped up in here on such a glorious day?' Her hair damp with sweat, her face muddied and dirty, Charlotte still pack a punch as she opened the fridge.

'We're fine,' Hamish snapped. 'Have you seen Bailey's potty? I was going to give the toilet training another go.'

'Why?' Charlotte blinked.

'Because that's what you do at this age.'

'What? Chase him around with a red potty? He thinks it's a game, you know.'

'I know,' Hamish groaned—exhausted from his attempts. 'But I've got the mothers at crèche all on at me offering me advice—you heard that Lucy, telling me about some bloody potty that plays music when he goes. Maybe I should buy one.'

'It would be cheaper to just say "good boy!"' Charlotte mused, 'but you know I *really* don't think the mothers at crèche could actually give two hoots whether Bailey's still in nappies or not.'

'And Helen said…' Hamish ignored her '…that she used to put table-tennis balls in the loo for target practice and her husband…' His voice trailed off as Charlotte just stood, buttered knife in hand, poised over the roll, an incredulous expression on her face.

'How bizarre!' Charlotte finally said, then with a little shrug started buttering the rolls as she chatted. 'Is there any reason it *has* to happen soon? I mean, have they suddenly found out he's a genius and he's going to be going to school next week and you don't want him to be the only kid in the school in nappies…?'

'Ha, ha,' Hamish said. 'You're not the one who has to chat to proud mums at crèche and find out their kids are already dry at night *and* sleeping through.'

'Good for them!' Charlotte shrugged. 'I love getting up to Bailey at night—we have great fun, don't we, darling?' She blew Bailey a kiss, who blew one back, and then carried on chatting. 'They're flirting with you, Hamish.'

'Who?'

'All those mums offering advice.'

'So Helen's flirting with me?'

'Well, not Helen,' Charlotte admitted. 'But I can assure you the others are. This Lucy—is she single?'

'I've no idea.'

'Well, I bet she is—or she fancies a bit of afternoon delight!'

'She was being nice,' Hamish protested.

'*Nice* people pop the potty in a plastic bag and leave it at the crèche with a little note with your name on the top, instead of...' Hand on hip, Charlotte stuck out her chest and batted her eyelashes as she lowered her voice. '"If you want it, Hamish, why don't you pop around get it?" And, oh, boy, would you get it.'

'Oh, no!'

'How about stripping off and going out for a picnic? I meant stripping off Bailey,' Charlotte explained patiently to his rather stunned expression, 'and bring him and the potty outside—you can give the poor carpet a break. I'll make a nice picnic.'

'We're fine,' Hamish retorted as Bailey jumped up in glee.

'Suit yourself.' Charlotte shrugged and after she'd gone Hamish sat with his face set, drumming his fingers loudly as Bailey grizzled to join his new friends, his little faced pressed against the glass door as Charlotte, the dog and the cat all headed off to the stables.

'Dar-dot!' he wailed, giving in and plonking his bottom on the floor and howling at the injustice of being left behind. 'Want Maisy!'

'How about some noodles?' Hamish offered his favourite lunch, but a whole morning of being mollified had had little effect and Bailey just quadrupled his efforts, knocking his noodles on the floor, screaming and kicking as Hamish lifted him over his shoulder and took him upstairs for a nap.

* * *

'No!' Hamish said firmly as Bailey tried to hurdle out of his cot, laying him back down for the umpteenth time then heading for the window to close the curtains and show Bailey that this time he meant business.

Only he didn't.

Because, staring out of the window, seeing her lying on the grass, staring up at sky as her pets dozed beside her, Hamish wanted to be out there, too. Wanted to be out enjoying the glorious afternoon instead of shut up inside, trying to pretend to Bailey that the stables didn't exist—not full ones anyway.

'Come on, mate.' Heaving Bailey out of the cot, as if turning off a tap, Bailey's tears halted. Realising he'd got his way, he even sat patiently on the kitchen floor as Hamish buttered a few rolls and grabbed some drinks and fruit from the fridge.

'What kept you?' Smiling, she didn't even open her eyes as, a little bit late but still very welcome, her lunch dates arrived.

'I was buttering rolls.'

'But I've already made plenty.'

'We'll have rolls for dinner, too, then,' Hamish answered, sitting down and pulling out a bag of grapes and offering them to Bailey. But the toddler's attention was elsewhere, pointing in glee at Scottie, who was poking his head over the stable door, and squealing in delight. And Hamish couldn't be bothered to argue any more. Fighting the fear that welled up in him when he pictured his beautiful son with the pony, he picked him up and headed over, letting him stroke Scottie's head and even letting Charlotte show Bailey how to hold out his hand flat. Hamish laughed out loud at Bailey's shocked but delighted expression as big lips nuzzled for the tiny grapes, watching his eyes shining brightly and his pink lips laughing, and for the first time in ages Hamish was treated to a rare glimpse of Emma in his son's expression

And it *had* been right to come down to the stables Hamish realised later, much later, when Bailey had had a thirty-second sit on Scottie's back and was now racing around on his tricycle, waving and beeping his horn to a very unfazed Scottie and Fitz each time he passed.

Hard, but right.

'Did you used to ride a lot? Before what happened with Emma, I mean?'

He was getting used to Charlotte's direct questions and this time he didn't really hesitate before answering.

'A bit.' Hamish nodded. 'I didn't really have anything to do with them till Emma came along—she was horse mad from the day she was born, I think. I'm not really the most horsy person.'

'He takes after Emma, then.' Charlotte nodded over at Bailey and never could she have known just how sweet those words were to hear.

'I guess he does. What about you—how old were you when you started riding?'

'Eight and absolutely petrified.'

'Did your parents make you?'

'Heavens no.' Charlotte gave a little giggle. 'My mum refused to get out of the car when she dropped me off for my lesson—worried she might get a bit of mud on her stilettos probably.'

'So how come you took it up?'

The bluest eyes in the world stared back at him, words for once not tumbling out. Instead, she lay back on the grass, stared up at the sky, her voice slightly pensive when it finally came. 'I just did.'

He stared at her for the longest time—and then over at Bailey. He split about a hundred pieces of grass into two with his thumbnail as that old feeling came back again—only stronger this time. Stronger and surer, and nothing he could say to himself could convince him otherwise. So she had strange dress sense at times, so she was ditzy and crazy and more often than not said the most inappropriate things—but she made him happy.

He stared around at his home, at his son, at his *life*— saw how much it had changed in the short time she'd been there, recognised now the feeling he'd had at the bottom of the stairs, a feeling that had been missing in his life for too long now.

Happiness.

'Tonight…' Hamish cleared his throat '…once Bailey's in bed, there's a nice curry house nearby. They deliver—'

'Sounds fab,' Charlotte interrupted, 'but I'm actually going out dancing tonight.'

'Dancing?'

'Come!' she offered easily. 'We'll have fun. Maybe Belinda could look after Bailey.'

'Better not!' Hamish answered. 'I think she needs a bit of a break.' He tried to sound as casual as she was, tried to tell himself that it didn't matter that she'd rather go out dancing on Saturday night with friends than stay in and share a take-away with a single father.

Only it did.

CHAPTER SIX

'I'M JUST going to check on the boys in the stable!' Charlotte grabbed an apple from the fruit bowl. Semi conscious, lying on the couch with a throw rug over him and all the chaos that a teething toddler created in the small hours surrounding him, Hamish was tempted to tell her to put more clothes on. She was in that bloody nighty and gumboots again, but, Hamish realised with a sigh, given it was seven in the morning, she had topped it with a massive old anorak. Truth be known, apart from her face, there was barely an inch of flesh showing—it was his imagination that was the problem! 'I saw you lying here when I got in last night. I hope I didn't wake you.'

'Only Bailey,' Hamish said, then regretted it. It wasn't her fault he was crazy about her, it wasn't her fault he'd missed her all night, jealous as hell and hating the lucky guy she was no doubt dancing with, it wasn't her fault that he was as grumpy as hell this morning.

'Did you get any real sleep at all?' Charlotte asked as she breezed over.

'What's that?' Hamish quipped.

'Oh, just something we lucky singles do!'

Leaning forward, she smothered a *nearly-finally-a-bloody-sleep-again* Bailey, who was lying on his chest, in a flurry of butterfly kisses, wafting her glorious fragrance and—Hamish wasn't sure if it was better or worse—unwittingly giving him a very good view of her left breast, causing Hamish to raise the throw rug a few generous inches higher. 'Are those lovely new teeth making Bailey's mouth sore?' Charlotte crooned as Bailey started to giggle.

'Do you mind?' Hamish snapped, wishing she'd get her luscious-looking breasts out of his face, wishing Bailey could somehow be magically transported to his cot and that it was just him she was leaning over and teasing with kisses…and wishing his erection would subside. 'He was nearly asleep!'

'Misery!' Charlotte grinned, unfortunately standing up and sticking out a pink tongue at him she waltzed out the door.

'Dar-dot!' Bailey sighed dreamily, finally deciding to sleep now that it was time to get up. Placing him in his cot, Hamish wondered whether to crawl into bed himself and grab a few hours or just plough on…

'Hamish!' He didn't know what he heard first, the crash of the kitchen door as it was pushed open loudly or Charlotte's urgent summons for help, but he took the staircase in two, maybe three strides. Colliding with her in the kitchen, his first instinct was to take her trembling hands.

'It's Sc-Scottie…' She stumbled the words out. 'I need you to get me a vet.'

'What's wrong?'

'Just call the vet!'

The home number of the vet was on speed dial—had been for years—one of those pieces of his old life that he hadn't yet found the heart to erase, and Hamish apologized to Nick's sleepy wife as she handed her husband the phone while Hamish ran to the stables.

'Can you come over soon, Nick?'

He had no idea what was wrong, but he knew from Charlotte's expression it was urgent. 'I've got an old pony here…'

Hamish stepped into the stable, entered a space he hadn't been in since Emma's death, and surprisingly she wasn't on his mind.

Instead, sick to the stomach at what surely lay ahead, he watched as Charlotte sank to her knees and buried her head in old Scottie's worried, pain-riddled face where he lay on the floor. Hamish took over, grabbing a blanket and covering him, doing what little he could to make him comfortable till help arrived…and trying to support Charlotte.

'The vet will be here soon.'

'Is he good?'

'He's great. His name is Nick—Emma swore by him.'

'Did you tell him it was serious?'

'He'll be here any moment.' God, he hoped she wasn't praying for a miracle here, Hamish thought as Charlotte closed her eyes and cuddled Scottie tighter, hoped to hell that Nick would get there soon.

He did, though it felt like for ever. As for Hamish,

there wasn't a single thing he could do. All she'd asked from him was a vet—and he'd delivered. But as she knelt holding her pet, though Hamish was more than used to dealing with distraught people, when it came to Charlotte he didn't have a clue, felt super-fluous almost as he stood there. She wasn't talking so he couldn't answer, she wasn't crying so he couldn't put out a hand to comfort her—she was like this little self-contained package on which he couldn't impinge.

Nick dealt with her well, though, and, Hamish decided, residents could learn a lot from vets.

There was no way animals could communicate, nothing to go on bar knowledge and instinct, and Nick had them in spades.

'He's got a lovely nature.' Examining the old boy well, expecting a bite or a kick, when he got neither all he could do was give a sad smile. 'Was he your first pony?'

'No.' Charlotte didn't look up, her head buried in Scottie's neck. 'I had Patch and then Nutmeg and then Scottie—he was an RDA horse.'

Hamish frowned as he tried to place the abbrevia-tion, but Nick got it in an instant. 'Riding for the disabled—no wonder he's such a sweetie. What happened here Charlotte?' He ran his finger along a scar on Scottie's abdomen. 'It looks fairly new.'

'Cancer!' Charlotte said through shivering teeth. 'In his colon. He had surgery last year—just for comfort—but he's done well, he even put on a bit of weight in the last few months. Do you think he's had a heart attack?'

Nick ran his stethoscope along the bloated stomach,

soothing and talking to the suffering animal as he did so.

'I'm not sure…' Nick admitted, hesitating before he broke the inevitable news, but Charlotte got there first.

'Don't shoot him!' For a second the two men looked at each other. There was no way this horse deserved a battery of tests before the inevitable end, but they soon realised they'd misinterpreted her: that it wasn't a question of prolonging his life, just rather more gently ending it. Standing up, dusting straw down from her nightdress, she ran a hand through her hair. 'Do what you have to do, but I don't want you to shoot him.'

'I won't. I'll anaesthetise him. Do you want to stay with him?'

'No, thank you.'

'Would you like us to give you a moment to say goodbye?'

'I already have.' Her teeth were really chattering now as she spoke and all Hamish wanted to do was put his arms around her, but something in her stance told him she wouldn't want it. 'Can I pay you now? Only I don't want a bill for this arriving in a couple of weeks— I'd rather just deal with it all today.'

'There's no charge,' Nick said as he stared at the withered pony and reminded himself all over again why he did this job. 'How many kids did this old boy make smile in his lifetime?'

'Lots!' Charlotte sniffed, and went to go but changed her mind, sinking to her knees for just one more fleeting second and kissing him goodbye for the last time.

* * *

It was horrible being back at the house.

Horrible watching her fill the kettle and chatting away as if nothing was going on outside.

'You must be exhausted—up all night with Bailey and then my dramas…' She filled his mug with hot water but forgot to put in the coffee, scooping in a ridiculous amount of sugar and then added so much milk that it slopped over the brim, chatted about everything and nothing as Hamish drank his tasteless brew.

Not even when the truck arrived did she waver—smiling at Bailey as he graced them with his presence, feeding him home-made pancakes and later chatting ten to the dozen as she cleaned the benches in the kitchen and a pale-faced Hamish bounced his son on his knee.

Only when the truck drove off did she waver.

Hamish gently put Bailey down and headed over to someone who today needed him just a little bit more—wrapping his arms around her frozen shoulders, holding her as the truck and its contents rumbled past.

'Daddy!' Bailey squealed in indignation, but Hamish didn't even hear it, holding her close, stroking her hair, and just blocking it all out when she needed it most.

'It's for the best really…' Sitting tiny on the sofa, legs tucked under her, her hand around a mug of hot chocolate, Hamish listened patiently as Charlotte rattled on.

It was just her way, Hamish told himself that night—just as he had maybe a hundred times that day.

She'd adored that pony, Hamish knew that, was sure that she *must* be bleeding inside, but apart from that small display of emotion when the truck had headed off,

Charlotte had just been…well, Charlotte. Chatty, happy and incredibly objective. 'He was just so-o old…' She gave a small sad smile. 'At least I won't have to worry about vet bills any more. He was costing me an absolute fortune.'

'That was where all your money went?' Hamish checked.

'All of it, and some I didn't have.' Charlotte nodded. 'I'd saved up for a new car—was just about to choose the colour, then he got cancer. He was in so much pain. I was going to have him destroyed, but then I wanted him to have just a few last weeks pain-free. The operation cost a fortune—then there was the aftercare. He lasted more than a year so it's been a running tap of vet's bills ever since.'

'He must have meant a lot to you…' Hamish attempted to get her to open up just a touch. 'To spend all that money when you knew….'

'He was past it? Oh, well, it's done now. I think I'll go to bed.'

'You'll be all right?'

'Of course,' Charlotte said, standing up.

'If you want to talk, we can. I could open a bottle of wine.'

'And watch me get maudlin over Scottie.' Charlotte shook her head. 'Look, I've known this day was coming for ages, Hamish. To tell the truth, it's actually a relief it's over.'

Heading up the stairs, Charlotte brushed her teeth and hair, carefully took off her make-up and then padded into the bedroom. Peeling off her clothes, she climbed into bed, staring dry-eyed at the ceiling, barely moving a muscle as ages later Hamish followed suit and came to bed.

And still she lay there, listening to Fitz whinnying into the night, calling out for his friend that had always been there, and his lonely call was almost more than she could bear.

'Don't!'

She actually said it out loud, got up and closed the window then climbed back into bed, willing sleep to come, willing her mind to think about the most banal of things...

Scared that if she started crying now, she'd never, ever stop.

Thumping the pillow and turning over, sleep still evaded her as ages later the phone trilled in the hallway and Bailey joined in with Fitz, calling out for his dad, when every other two-year-old was calling out for Mum...

God, she hated this cruel world sometimes.

'Charlotte.' There was a small rap at the door then it opened. 'That was the hospital. I'm not on call but they've just been alerted to a house fire on the outskirts of town—it sounds nasty.'

'Go!' Charlotte called, her voice not quite as clear as usual, and it had nothing to do with the fact it was the middle of the night.

'Can I put the light on?'

She didn't want him to put the light on, didn't want him to check that she was okay to look after Bailey, but unusually he didn't await her response, just pushed the door open farther and flicked on the light, watching as her pale features blanched at the intrusion, trying not to notice as she sat up and huddled the sheet around her that she was naked beneath it.

'I said you'd come in, too—I hope that's okay. It's a family of six. I've rung Belinda and I'm taking Bailey over there.'

She pulled on her uniform in a matter of seconds as Hamish tried to gently rouse Bailey from his slumber, loading him into the Jeep and thankfully taking the keys and driving.

Belinda was in her driveway, huddled in her dressing gown, clearly more than used to this type of late-night drama.

'Good luck,' she called out as she took charge of Bailey and closed the door.

'Poor little mite.'

'He's fine,' Charlotte soothed, but her heart wasn't really in it, seeing firsthand what the two of them had to regularly endure rammed home again how impossible Hamish's work situation was.

And yet...

Looking sideways she saw his strong profile silhouetted in the darkness, his mind already on the job ahead. She'd seen him in action, seen him rolling up his sleeves in Emergency, seen him lecturing his juniors, marvelled at the depths of his knowledge, and she knew, if tragedy struck her family tonight...Hamish Adams was the doctor she'd want greeting them at the emergency room door....

How could he give it away?

And if he did—what a waste of an amazing talent.

'Not what you needed, huh.' Catching her staring, Hamish glanced over as he drove.

'I'm sure the family whose house was on fire would say the same thing.'

'Were you always this tough?' Flicking on the indicator, he turned the car into the driveway of the hospital and both their eyes scanned the foyer for activity, both wondering how many fire trucks, how many ambulances would have beaten them there.

Both suddenly sick to their stomach when there wasn't a single one.

'Hamish!' Helen's voice was brisk as they raced across the foyer, turning off the phone in her hand and greeting them in the brightly lit ambulance bay. 'I was just calling your mobile.' She ran a hand through wiry grey hair, her sixty-year-old face tired and heavily lined thanks to an unwelcome but compulsory stint of night duty and the news she was about to impart. 'You won't be needed after all.' Pulling her navy cardigan tighter around her, she didn't quite meet his eyes as she spoke. 'Ambulance Control just called through—there weren't any survivors.'

'The firefighters?' Hamish clipped. 'Any injuries there—smoke inhalation—?'

'No.' Helen shook her head. 'They couldn't even get close enough to get in. They're just dousing it now. The coroner's making his way to the scene and no doubt a few news channels are, too.

'I'm sorry for calling you in, both of you...' She gave a small nod to Charlotte. 'I just thought—'

'Always call me, Helen,' Hamish interrupted. 'I'm just sorry we weren't needed.'

It was the longest drive home, no Bailey to pick up, no glimpses of normal to force a break from the horror of what had tonight taken place. The adrenaline that had spurred them out of bed and into the night markedly absent as they drove in silence, both locked in their own thoughts. And for Charlotte it was hell—like the cord being pulled on a chainsaw, her mind kept attempting to whir into angry frenzy.

'I might just have that glass of wine after all!' Her voice was high as she headed for the fridge. 'I'm not on till midday. Do you want one?'

'Better not—I have to pick up Bailey then be back there by eight. Go ahead, though.'

She did.

The tiniest of drinkers, like a child taking some awful medicine, she took a sip and then another, hating the tears that were starting to build, hating that he noticed.

'It's okay to be upset.'

'I know!' A jagged smile ripped through her strained features. 'It kinds of put my day into perspective.'

'It doesn't work like that, Charlotte, and you know it…grief compounds grief with all you've been through today….'

'You can't compare a family of six to a pony,' Charlotte snapped. 'You can't even begin to compare a family of six with a *blind…stupid…old…pony*…' She stopped herself then, the chainsaw that had spluttered into life cutting out just before it let rip. But Hamish wasn't going to give in—this, the most raw he had seen her, the most *honest* she had been—a glimpse of the real Charlotte he knew was there finally coming to the fore, and he wasn't going to lose her now.

'Who's comparing?' Hamish said softly, taking her tense shoulder in his hands. 'If we lived by those rules then losing Emma shouldn't hurt that much. I'm just saying—'

'Well, don't!' She snarled the words out, her hand raised to push him away to run for the stairs, to get to her room and take off the beastly uniform that hadn't even been needed, or run out to the stables and bury her head in Fitz's neck, wanted to howl out loud for all the people who were lonely and sad and scared tonight.

All the people who were missing someone they loved.

Cassie!

The cord was out on the chainsaw, her mind buzzing with grief that she could never ever share, and *nothing* was going to obliterate it, not a glass of wine, not some carefully chosen words of comfort…

Nothing!

His lips on hers were as unexpected as they were blissful.

Calm creeping in when surely it should be the opposite!

His full mouth pressing on hers, hushing the pain in her mind.

Strong hands moving from her shoulder and pulling her into his strong warmth.

And that teasing taste made her hungry for more, his

tongue cool and welcome as it slipped between her lips, and it was such bliss to be held, to be held by someone so strong, to have someone just take over the reins for a little bit and not just someone, but Hamish…

'Oh, Charlotte…' His voice was a rasp as he pulled back, questions, guilt perhaps flickering in those guarded hazel eyes, but she didn't want to hear how impossible it was, didn't care about the regret that might hit tomorrow, because the glimmer of bliss he had brought her tonight had been so unexpected, her pain so seemingly impossible to eradicate, yet with one kiss he had.

'Why shouldn't we be happy,' Charlotte whispered, 'even if it's just tonight?'

She didn't know how she got to his bedroom. Vaguely she could remember them kissing all the way up the stairs, her uniform, his clothes strewing the hallway like a trail to the bedroom, but never, never in a million years would she forget the beauty of the moment they faced each other naked—the sheer heaven of his toned body just a breath away as he stared down at her, his tender eyes caressing her, warming her, and even if they weren't touching, for now it was more than enough.

'You're beautiful, Charlotte.' There was this hint of wonder in his voice and she wasn't insecure enough to misinterpret it—knew with blinding certainty that he'd never figured on saying it in this room to a woman who wasn't Emma.

'So are you.'

He kissed her again, only not on the lips, burying his

face in her neck, his hot mouth working each exquisitely tender angle, till there was no where to go except closer.

His body pressed against her quite simply felt divine—just so, so male, Charlotte realised with a little sigh.

'We're so different.' Pulling back, she stared back at him.

'I know,' Hamish rasped. 'I know on paper we could never ever work, but—'

'Not in that way.' Charlotte giggled, nervous and excited at the same time. Running a tentative hand over his thighs, she told him a little more of what she was thinking. 'I *like* that you're hairy, only not too much.'

'And I like that you're smooth,' Hamish countered, his own hand moving not quite so quickly and lingering for way too long on her bottom.

'What about this bit?' Charlotte whispered, guiding his mouth to breasts that had teased him for ever, closing her eyes in bliss as he contemplated the difference, utterly breathless when finally Hamish delivered his verdict. 'Way more interesting than mine.'

'Are you sure?' He thought she was offering a licence for him to continue, only he was wrong, his hand involuntarily scrunching her hair as she lavished him with the same amount of attention he had bestowed, his erection dancing unattended as her tongue caressed his nipples, as her little sharp teeth nibbled—and just as he was about to explode, just as he was about to push her on the bed and make very quick but very glorious love to her, Charlotte looked up and the flirting the teasing ended.

'Will we be okay?'

'Way better than okay,' Hamish promised, and she chose to believe him, chose to partake in the glorious dance unfolding as they became more than a man and a woman, but a couple, tasted each other, adored each other, sure enough now to know this was happening, to lie on the bed together, to drift onto cotton and feel his skin next to her, to drown in the exquisite balm of his foreplay, to feel his hands stroke away the pain and take her elsewhere... And to do the same for him.

And there was no rush, because they had each other for as long as was needed, the train of grief pausing at the station for as long as was required, and they were both so grateful just to step off for now.

He was just glorious, though incredibly demanding, but, then, so was she, shivering in delight as he tenderly explored her, her bottom wiggling in his palm as she breathlessly urged him on.

Today, tonight, had been agony, but it faded away when finally he took her, filling her, holding her, loving her, and it was easier to give in than to fight it, easier to trust him and love him right back, her orgasm so intense, so consuming it could have blocked out the sun if needed.

Yet if it was bliss for Charlotte, then for Hamish it was more.

More than he could have ever hoped or dared to feel again.

And it wasn't just the sex that was brilliant, it was all of it.

All of her.

The bed the right size with her there beside him.

Spooning her warm, flushed body into his, feeling her relax against him as sleep drifted in, he stared into the darkness and tried to fathom the impossible—a woman who wasn't Emma was lying beside him and he felt relaxed, happy for the first time in ages.

A woman called Charlotte was lying in his arms and all it felt was right.

CHAPTER SEVEN

WHOEVER said things always seemed better in the morning hadn't woken to the wedding picture of Hamish's late wife smiling down at her—or felt the tension creep into his body as he'd stirred beside her—the arm that had held her close through the night pulling her towards him as naturally as breathing then stiffening as his mind no doubt skipped to its rude awakening and the realisation that she wasn't Emma. Okay, Charlotte reasoned, he didn't run out of the bed screaming and, sure, he'd tried to kiss her and smile and pretend he didn't regret it, but the air was so thick with guilt she swore she could taste it.

'I'm just going to have a shower…' He climbed out of bed and tried hard to look her in the eye, but failed spectacularly. 'I'm running a bit late…'

'Sure.' Charlotte's smile was as wide as it was false, turning off like a tap the second the bedroom door closed, and then, when she heard the taps safely running, Charlotte made her move.

Emma's *clothes* were still in the wardrobe, her shoes

lined up on the floor as if daring Charlotte to even *try* to step into them.

The room surely the same as she'd left it on the day she'd died—it was as if Emma had just popped out to the shops, or was away for a couple of days, and for Charlotte it was like being punched in the stomach as realisation hit.

Hamish hadn't move on an inch.

Inherently nosy, though entirely without malice, Charlotte opened Emma's bedside drawer. The familiar cover of a book Charlotte had enjoyed a couple of years ago stared back at her, a book that only a woman would either read or understand, and Charlotte picked it up, tears welling in her eyes as she saw the bookmarked page near the back of the book and read where Emma had got up to, wishing for her just another night in bed, a few more hours so she could have found out the end. She carefully replaced the book. Heading to the dresser and picking up a ring that lay in a little glass dish on there, Charlotte stared at yet another photo and somehow felt as if she should say something.

'He didn't mean it…' She stared back at Emma, took in the ripe, pregnant body dressed in nothing more than a bikini, stared into emerald-green eyes that were crinkling with a smile as she faced the camera, and Charlotte was in no doubt that Hamish had been the person who had taken the photo, the captured moment just so intimate, so, so loving, quite simply it couldn't have been anyone else. 'He just misses you and last night…' Charlotte swallowed. 'Well, he must have been hurting just a little bit more.'

He'd tell her to leave.

Of that she was certain.

Oh, not this morning. Hamish was way too much of a gentleman to kiss and run—but unless she dealt with this quickly, in a week or a month she'd be out of here…last night had been too much, too soon.

Way too much!

Charlotte closed her eyes for a second—recalled their love-making, the heady intimacies they had shared that had been so much more than sex.

God, what would Cassie do? And for the first time her sister's perspective evaded her—Charlotte really didn't know what her sister would have done. Fifteen-year-olds had major crushes, fifteen-year-olds *thought* they were in love…

Twenty-eight-year-olds *knew* when they were.

She loved him.

Not fancy, or like, or maybe, or possibly a bit more…

Some time, somehow, living with her handsome, detached boss and his gorgeous, loving little boy she had actually fallen in love with him.

Dropping the ring back into the dish, as realisation hit, Charlotte actually averted her eyes from the photo—felt more than a fraction of the guilt that was surely drenching Hamish now, her mind racing for answers, wishing she could somehow erase last night, so that Hamish didn't hate her this morning.

Wishing she could buy herself just a little more time so that maybe, just maybe he could come to love her, too.

She had to deal with this—and soon.

* * *

'Whoops!' Pouring water onto instant coffee, Charlotte gave Hamish a beaming smile as he came into the kitchen. Dressed and smelling divine, he was drying his hair on a towel and trying to pretend things were normal between them.

'What do you mean, "Whoops"?'

'Tell me you're not thinking the same…' Still she smiled as she watched his Adam's apple bob up and down.

'We can talk tonight…' He put down the towel and started organising Bailey's nappy bag, but Charlotte didn't want to talk about it tonight, knew that a few hours of unchecked guilt would have Hamish coming up with a solution she didn't want to hear.

'It's okay, Hamish. I'm not expecting a dozen roses to arrive before my shift. Last night was great and everything, but we both know—'

'Know what?' Finally he was looking at her and never had she struggled more to be ditzy and dizzy.

'That last night probably shouldn't have happened. Last night were both feeling wretched—you missing Emma, me upset over Scottie, and then the fire… It was just one of those things.' She gave a little shrug, tried as hard as she could to convince him that just because of what had happened last night, the little world they had created, the world they were *starting* to create, didn't have to end. Her eyes strayed to the fistful of nappies he was holding because it was easier than looking at him, but he misconstrued the meaning. 'All a bit too much responsibility for you, Charlotte? Tell you what…' His voice was clipped as he spoke, his eyes narrowing as he eyed her standing there, still not looking at him. 'Next time you can't sleep, why don't you do us both a favour?' Bypassing the coffee she had made, his hand pushed the barely touched bottle of wine she had opened last night towards her. 'Just have another glass of this instead.'

'So you're sure there's nothing between you two…'

Frowning, Hamish stared intently at the X-ray on the lightbox—not that there was any need. The second he'd snapped it up he'd seen the problem—staring boldly back at him between the jumble of old fractures and calcification was a new Colles' fracture, which meant plaster, elevate, back in twenty-four hours for review. But for his sudden scrutiny it might just as well have been a multiple trauma's CT up on the screen!

'Sorry?'

'Charlotte Porter.' Cameron blushed. 'I was going to ask her out again. I just wanted to make sure… I mean…' He was stumbling with embarrassment. 'I know that you two are living together.'

'She's my babysitter,' Hamish snapped. 'My live-in babysitter—so, yes, I suppose, effectively we live together.'

'I just wanted to be sure that you weren't…' Cameron was practically purple now and the easiest thing would have been to put him out of his misery, to tell him the truth—that after her little speech that morning there was absolutely nothing between him and Charlotte Porter, that she was just a live-in help, yet he couldn't quite manage it.

When he'd woken that morning to find her beside him, he'd been so loaded with guilt at what had taken place he'd barely even been able to look at her. Only his guilt wasn't solely reserved for Emma, an extremely generous serving had been cut for Charlotte.

She'd been so raw, so vulnerable last night... He should have had more control, should have gone to bed instead of...

Hell, to think he'd been worried that *she'd* think he'd taken advantage of her, had guiltily acknowledged that maybe he had just a touch. It had never entered his head that it had been Charlotte taking advantage of him! It had never even crossed his mind when he'd come down the stairs ready to tell her he was sorry, that if she thought he'd rushed things last night then he was more than happy to take things a little more slowly, that she'd be standing grinning at the kettle and chalking it down to experience!

'She's a fun girl.' Cameron gulped. 'She's so upbeat and happy...'

'We're supposed to be doing the fracture clinic,' Hamish tartly pointed out, 'not discussing the supposed assets of my live-in help.'

'I just wanted to be sure that's all she is.' Cameron flashed a nervous smile. 'I just wanted to check—I mean, I know you're older than her and that...' He gave a small cough. 'Well, what with your baby and everything, you'd be a petty unlikely couple. I just don't want to step on the boss's toes and all that.'

'Please!' Hamish's voice was dry. 'There's nothing between us and, as *old* as you think I might be, I'm neither Charlotte's lover nor her father—she doesn't need my permission to date.' Slapping a red spot on the X-ray, he turned to his resident. 'Where's the fracture?'

His frown deepened as Cameron floundered. 'Come on—surely you can see it? No one could miss this.'

'There…' Cameron's shaking finger pointed out the irregularity—and Hamish felt a tinge of guilt. Thanks to osteoporosis, Anna Cleveland's X-rays were to most newly trained eyes pretty indecipherable, but Cameron had spotted the most recent deformity.

'So, what now?'

'Plaster, elevate, analgesia, review in twenty-four hours. Anything I've missed?' Cameron added nervously, when Hamish didn't respond to his treatment plan.

'Nothing,' Hamish answered with more than heavy dash of irony then, as Cameron beat a hasty exit, he added, 'You've missed absolutely nothing!'

'Er, is there a nurse who works here called Charlotte?' A good-looking guy standing in front of him, holding a bunch of flowers and a vast tin of chocolates, did nothing to improve Hamish's already black mood— why the hell didn't she just set up a dating agency at the reception desk?

'Charlotte?' Hamish frowned and pretended he had no idea who he was talking about. 'I'm not sure if there is—you'll have to ask at Reception.'

'Hamish!' Vince King came running towards them, tucking away his mobile phone and pumping a bemused Hamish's hands and explaining things to his son. 'That's the Dr Adams I was telling you about,

Ronan.' He beamed over at Hamish. 'We're just on our way home—I told Ronan all that you did for him, for me, too! We just wanted to come and say thank you before we left.'

'Oh, my!' Strange that on a day like this, he was reminded again why Emergency would be so hard to leave, why he couldn't bring himself to work in Admin or stand in front of a group of medical students and attempt to prepare them for times like this…because standing six feet two, staring directly back at him, Ronan was almost unrecognisable as the man who had lain unconscious and lifeless in Resus. A man who had been so very close to death just a short time ago.

Not to Charlotte, though—a can of cola in hand, she gave a loud wolf whistle as she approached that had them all jumping.

'Look at you!' She grinned in wonder. 'I hardly recognised you with your clothes on.'

'This is Charlotte.' Hamish introduced them just a touch sheepishly, now he had realised just who her admirer actually was, watching as an embarrassed Ronan handed the bunch of flowers to an embarrassed Vince, who then handed the flowers to a delighted Charlotte and then, after a moment's deliberation, gave in and hugged her.

'You were great that day,' Vince said in a gruff voice. 'You listened to what I was telling you—then, even when the news wasn't great you gave it to me straight. I really appreciate it.'

'You're more than welcome. Gosh…' she added,

staring over at her ex-patient in wonder. 'You're a walking miracle, do you know that?'

'I've been told that several times,' Ronan nodded. 'Apparently my gumboots saved me—if I hadn't been wearing them, I've been told I'd have been cooked like a sausage on a barbecue.'

'Any lasting injuries?' Hamish checked.

'Some.' Ronan nodded. 'I've got to come in for some more tests in a few weeks—and I've got some nasty burns on my feet which need to be dressed twice a day…' Only then did Hamish notice the oversized runners covering his undoubtedly heavily bandaged feet as Ronan continued, 'But I'm not complaining.' He gave a low laugh. 'Not ever again. I *know* how lucky I am to be here!'

'And don't you ever forget it,' Charlotte said, her breathy voice suddenly serious. She gave him one of her endless supply of hugs. 'Not for a single moment— do you hear me?'

But the magic wand that had graced Ronan that morning still hadn't found its way to the paediatric ward. Despite intensive treatment for his skin condition and a lot of work behind the scenes with the school, psychologists and social workers, a forlorn face greeted Charlotte as she popped in on her afternoon tea-break. Andy looking lost and alone all over again now his new-found friend had been discharged and sent home.

'I love your new glasses!'

'Thanks.' Andy barely looked up, his little face working up to cry, and Charlotte could guess why—the intensive treatment had made a vast improvement to his skin, regular chats with the child psychologist and social worker had addressed some of the tough issues of his bullying and anxiety but, for Andy, the hard yards were about to begin. 'I go home tomorrow.' He gave her a worried frown. 'Then back to school on Wednesday.'

'How do you feel about that?'

'Dunno.' Andy shrugged. 'A bit nervous.'

'It's okay to be nervous.'

'The teachers have spoken to them—the bullies,' Andy added, and Charlotte nodded. 'And Mum said they've spoken to their parents as well.'

'That's good!'

'How can it be good?' Andy shouted loudly, letting out a little of what he was holding in, and Charlotte glanced around, catching the ward nurse's eye and gesturing to the curtain. After a nod, Charlotte stood up and closed them around his bed as Andy carried on. 'They said I wasn't to tell anyone,' Andy sobbed, angry and scared and not knowing what to do. 'What if it made things worse?'

'It's all out in the open now, Andy, and it might just have things a whole lot better,'

'Or a whole lot worse,' he sobbed, refusing to be comforted.

'Could it be much worse than it already was?' Charlotte questioned gently.

'Maybe. What if they still don't stop?'

'Then you have to brave and tell someone.'

'I did that,' Andy gulped. 'I told you.'

'And you did the right thing,' Charlotte said gently

but firmly. 'I know it was the hardest thing in the world to do and I think you've been so brave. And I know you don't think grown-ups can possibly understand, that you don't think anyone can understand…'

'I'm scared it will all start again.'

'It might,' Charlotte said, watching as he blinked at her honesty. 'Only this time you're not going to hope it will go away, you're not going to hope things will get better or that they'll move on. You're going to speak up and out—every time, no matter how hard it is at first.'

'Did you?'

'In the end.' Charlotte nodded. 'Andy, I'm sure those boys are in a lot of trouble, the school was very worried when they found out all that's happened…'

'What do can they do? Ooh, you just don't get it.' Andy shook his head and rolled over in bed, turning his back on her. 'And I know that you lied to me…' Andy ripped off his new glasses and tossed them on the locker.

'When did I lie to you?' Charlotte frowned. 'I've come to see you every time I said I would.'

'Not about that…when you said you knew how I felt, when you said you knew how scary it was to be picked on, well, I know that you lied to me.'

'I wish I had been lying,' Charlotte said. 'I wish I had been, but I wasn't. I *was* telling the truth, Andy.' She looked at his serious, doubting face and suddenly it was imperative that he believe her—imperative that this little, scared boy could know that someone big and grown up, and in his eyes beautiful, could one day have visited the place he inhabited now. 'Look, I have to go back down to Emergency, but tonight when my shifts finished I'll come up and talk to you.' Charlotte took a deep breath. 'Really talk to you—and I'll tell you how it was for me.'

'Promise?'

She hesitated for a second before nodding—oh, she couldn't lumber this little guy with all of it, but a slice of her truth might just help.

'I promise.'

CHAPTER EIGHT

'SORRY, baby.' Burying her head in Fitz's neck, Charlotte hugged him tightly. 'You must be wondering what on earth has happened, what with me not coming to see you, a new home, and no Sco—' She couldn't say his name yet, but she'd work on it.

She'd ended up staying for ages at the hospital, telling her story to Andy, and whatever psychologist had come up with the theory that exploring one's past was healthy clearly hadn't had much of one! The hours spent talking to Andy had been followed by an hour sitting in the deserted staff canteen, utterly drained and drinking cola, trying to summon up the mental and physical energy to drive. By the time she'd got home she had been just too exhausted to drag herself down to the stables. Still, Hamish clearly had thought to. Fitz was wearing his rug and she made a mental note to thank him—or not.

He'd been downright rude at work—had been in bed when she'd come in last night and had recoiled as if she were poison when they'd collided on the landing at two in the morning, Hamish racing to get to Bailey, Charlotte racing to get to the loo.

Staring over at the house, seeing the light flick on in the kitchen, for the zillionth time Charlotte wondered how she should be with him, gulping at how difficult things were between them right now and wondering if they would ever get better.

Maybe she should move out, Charlotte thought as she saddled up Fitz. Maybe if they just saw each other at work, they could sort of start over. Now that Scottie wasn't burning her money, she could move back to the youth hostel, work an extra shift for Fitz's fees and maybe put Maisy and Eric into kennels till she found somewhere that didn't mind pets.

But who'd look after Bailey?

Someone would—of course they would—but it wouldn't be her, and that hurt, hurt more than she dared admit.

Hurt as much as, maybe even more than, the prospect of losing Hamish.

In just a short time she'd truly come to love him— his cheeky smile, his complete adoration of her—sort of a gorgeous mini-Hamish, only without the scowl! She could barely look at Bailey without breaking down, furious with herself for messing things up and dreading having to let go.

Fitz was as unenthusiastic at the prospect of an early morning ride as his owner. Left out in the paddock, he had grown fat and lazy and, to boot, seemed to have forgotten all he'd learnt. It took more than a few kicks and a good hit with her crop just to get him to walk a few steps.

'Come on, Fitz!' Charlotte urged, her legs tired and heavy and already just a bit out of breath, and they were only a few steps through the gate. 'Come on!' She shouted, summoning her energy and giving him the boot, but it wasn't the deft kick from his owner that had him moving, but the very unfamiliar sound of her angry voice that had his fat body shooting into a rapid trot. Charlotte, caught by surprise, lost her left stirrup, her weight tipping to the right in the saddle for a moment as Fitz surged on, and it took all the energy she didn't have this morning to right herself, before pulling him to a halt and then jumping down.

'I'm sorry.' She was nearly crying as she spoke, tired and scared and more than a bit angry at herself for being so mean when he was missing his friend. 'That was all my fault, Fitz, not yours—you've had a rotten few days and so have I. We'll have a gentle walk after my shift…' Taking a few deep breaths, Charlotte willed herself calm, took him by the reins and started to walk back to the stables. It seemed to take for ever. Even untacking him was an effort and for the first time she actually wondered if it wasn't just the rotten few days that were making her feel so awful…

'Not this week,' Charlotte moaned. The *last* thing she needed was a cold or worse—she had just way too much on. Glimpsing her week ahead, it seemed was insurmountable. She was tempted to just head to home and bed and pull the sheets over her heads till the whole blessed thing was over.

If she still had a home, that was!

Muddy and grubby, dressed in faded jodhpurs and a jumper full of holes, to Bailey she was beautiful.

'Dar-dot!' Banging his spoon in delight as she came in, he struggled to get her attention.

'Oh, hi, Bailey...' Charlotte gave Bailey a distracted smile, and watching her turn her back on a little guy who loved her, just putting a slice of bread into the toaster and watching *it* rather than talking to *him*, was, for Hamish, the hardest part.

Seeing Bailey whining and miserable, already way too used to her usually lavish attention, Hamish could see in his hurt face that he was completely unable fathom what he'd done wrong, wondering why she wasn't coming over to the highchair and pinching one of his toast soldiers as she usually did, why she wasn't begging his dad to turn to the horoscope page in the newspaper. And when she continued to stare at the blessed toaster Hamish was sorely tempted to get up and tap her on the shoulder and tell her exactly what he thought of her behaviour!

But what would be the point?

Sure, he might guilt her into feigning a few more kisses for Bailey, then he'd have to sit back and watch as his little heart was broken all over again.

'Come on, Bailey.' Hamish turned the highchair round more to face him. 'Let's finish your breakfast.'

'Thanks for settling Fitz last night.' Yawning, she looked over. 'I got stuck at work.'

Funny that Belinda had called him last night from a casual evening shift in A and E out of sheer boredom because the place had been unusually empty!

'I thought things were quiet there last night…' he started, then stopped himself. What was the point? 'How was your ride?'

'Great…' Charlotte answered, and he watched in silence as she buttered her toast then came over to the table where he was frowning, seriously wondering now if everything she had ever said had been a lie.

He'd *seen* her nearly fall from the kitchen window, had looked up as he'd finished slicing up Bailey's toast and with heart in mouth had seen Fitz start to panic as Charlotte had briefly lost control. Seeing her shift in the saddle and that brief struggle to right herself, his first instinct had been to rush out…

Not that she'd have appreciated his concern, Hamish thought darkly.

'Dar-dot!' As a last resort Bailey held out a half-chewed toast soldier towards her, but she barely looked up. He just didn't get her—fifteen minutes ago she'd been with Fitz, gently walking him back, showering him with the hugs and kisses, yet now here she sat, snubbing the innocent victim in this grown-up mess, and Hamish knew for his son's sake he had to step in— had to try to and wean Bailey off her, before his beloved Dar-dot disappeared forever!

'It's Alicia's birthday today.'

'Alicia.' Charlotte frowned.

She cared more about her bloody animals than humans, Hamish thought savagely, or, at least, as long as they were alive! 'My niece,' he said tightly. 'Anyway, Belinda's going to pick Bailey up from crèche and have him over for a birthday tea, so you don't have to worry about collecting him or anything.'

'Fine.' She put down the slice of toast that she'd barely nibbled the edges of and refilled her glass of orange juice which she'd downed in one. 'You know, I'm not really that hungry. I think I'll go and have my shower. You get dressed, young man.' She smiled over at Bailey who, starved of attention from her, promptly melted. 'I'll be down in a bit to take you in.'

'No need,' Hamish said, unclipping Hamish and picking him up from his highchair. 'I'm starting a bit later this morning—I'll take him in with me.'

'Fine.' Charlotte gave a tight smile.

'Good.' Hamish didn't even attempt one back, just headed upstairs and dressed Bailey, taking an inordinate amount of time to do so, waiting till she was in the shower before driving to work and taking Bailey into crèche.

'Hamish!' Lucy stopped talking to whoever it was she was talking to and, a plastic bag in her hand, made her way over. 'The musical potty I was telling you about. I was just about to leave it for you.'

'Thanks!' Hamish actually managed a smile, though it was more a wry one at Charlotte than at the woman standing in front of him. 'That's really *nice* of you.'

'Actually, I was hoping to catch you.' Despite a *lot* of foundation, there was a blush creeping up her cheeks. 'Look, I know you're on your own. I am, too. I was thinking we should get together sometimes…'

'Yeah,' Hamish said carefully, 'I was thinking I should have a few of Bailey's little friends over one weekend.'

'I wasn't talking about the kids!'

And maybe he should be feeling flattered, Hamish thought as he made his way back to the department, but all he felt was…

Tired.

Sitting at the nurses' station, he flicked through the internal post, and now that Charlotte wouldn't be doing it for him, he had a quick flick through the internally advertised vacancies. Helen chatted on, but he wasn't even pretending to listen.

God, did everyone think it was that easy? He could almost hear their thought processes, had seen the eyebrows raised when Charlotte had moved in. *Oh, well, it's been eighteen months now, it's probably about time he started to move on…*

But it wasn't about sex.

Or finding a wife or a mother for Bailey.

And it definitely wasn't loneliness or boredom—he'd give his back teeth even to glimpse the luxury of those two.

It was about missing Emma and now missing Charlotte.

Missing two beautiful women who had at different times and stages graced his life and trying to work his way through it.

Maybe he should try and date his way through his misery, Hamish mused, take up every one of those thinly veiled offers and try screwing his way out of this hell—after all, it seemed to work for Charlotte!

The ringing of the emergency phone snapped him out of his misery, and for once he beat Helen to answering it, listening to the details from the ambulance control as Helen hovered close by.

'Snakebite.' Hamish said grimly, hanging up the receiver and pressing the bell on the desk that alerted all resus staff to make their way over. 'Definite snakebite to the leg in a twelve-year-old boy. Collapsed, hypotensive, he'll be here in ten!'

For a twelve-year-old, Jordan Reece was a rather big boy and although being overweight wasn't considered healthy—it was one of the factors that might just his life. Venomous snakes were found in Victoria, especially in rural areas, and the hot, dry weather was doing its part in bringing them out. Jordan had been bitten on the calf by an unknown breed of snake while messing around at playtime in the sheds at the back of his school, but prompt attention of friends in alerting the teachers and immediate first aid applied by the school nurse had been invaluable.

A pressure bandage had been applied and his limb immobilised, but even with the correct first aid treatment for a snakebite, by the time he was in the helicopter and on his way to hospital he had collapsed, arriving in Emergency with ominous signs—dangerously low blood pressure and convulsing.

'Right.' Hamish never missed a beat—ordering bloods, fluids and drugs, then deciding to anaesthetise and intubate as the team worked hard to stabilise this desperately ill child.

'Sounds like a brown snake,' the paramedic called out as Hamish swabbed the wound on Jordan's leg. The venom detection kit was needed to confirm the breed of snake that had struck. 'One of the kids got a pretty good look at him and knows the breeds.'

'Not enough to go on.' Hamish shook his head. The VDK kit wasn't used to determine whether or not antivenom was required but to confirm the type that was needed. Giving antivenom was a medical decision based on the presentation of the victim and in this case the half-hour wait for the VDK test to come back was just too long. The administration of both brown and tiger snake antivenom, was the choice Hamish made— first pre-medicating Jordan to reduce the risk of anaphylactic reaction, before commencing the infusion of the vital antivenom.

'What's the bed status like in ICU?' It was the first time Hamish had spoken for half an hour without giving an order, but slowly things were starting to calm down, at least for young Jordan. For the staff, the drama wasn't anywhere near over—especially when the anaesthetist gave his familiar wry smile with his single word anwswer.

'Guess!'

'What were they thinking?' Helen droned on as Hamish sat stuck on hold on the phone. 'Or did you even stop to think?'

'Oh, so it's my fault.' Hamish whistled through his teeth. 'The fact there isn't a single ICU bed in the state for a twelve-year-old is solely down to me?'

'Well, all the meetings you went to, all the hours and hours this department had to go without a consultant while you were up in Admin, supposedly working out this blessed "transition phase". Did you not even once stop to think *where* we were going to be putting all the extra patients we would be getting?'

Probably not, Hamish was tempted to answer—tempted to remind her he'd been at Emma's funeral a couple of weeks before the details of the ICU transition phase had been decided, tempted to say it but not wanting to pull out the sympathy card.

And more than a little bit angry with himself because, like it or not, Helen was just a little bit right.

Not that he'd tell her that now, though!

He adored Helen, considered her way more than a long-time colleague, but when she had a bee in her bonnet she was possibly the most irritating person he had met—and she had a full hive in there now! 'There are more than a ninety new beds in the hospital,' Hamish hissed, 'and there are two more new wards opening next month. Now, if you don't mind, I'm trying to find this child an ICU bed—preferably somewhere within the state.'

'But, that's exactly my point—there are only two new *adult* ICU beds and *one* more paediatric.'

'And another three opening next week.' Hamish gritted his teeth and willed the bed manager to answer his page and sort this blessed mess out, knowing that if he lost it now, he would explode. The hell of working with, living with and trying to avoid Charlotte *and* keep an even state of mind was proving an impossible feat!

'Oh, well, that's good news.' Helen's voice dripped with sarcasm. 'But it does nothing for this child here now with a snakebite.' And though he knew from experience that Helen was always especially anxious where very sick children were concerned, that this was just her way of letting off a bit of steam as to all the changes she had been forced to endure, Hamish could have cheerfully strangled her as she twittered on . 'All this phasing in and phasing out—I'll tell you who's fazed!'

'Thank you very much!' Hanging up the phone, he turned to Helen and fixed her with a steely stare. 'There's a bed coming up at City Hospital—their transfer team is out on a retrieval right now so I'm going in the helicopter with him.' Helen opened her mouth to speak but she rather rapidly changed her mind, something in Hamish's stance, his voice telling her she'd pushed him just a touch too far. 'And, yes, that means I'll need a nurse and, yes, I know it will mess up your roster, and that we'll have to arrange cover from the wards or, worse still, the agency, which will mess up your budget, and that then she'll no doubt have not a shred of experience in emergency. I know all that so you don't have to tell me—now, can you, please, just arrange an experienced nurse escort?'

'Of course.' Helen flushed, pouncing on Charlotte as she walked past the nurses' station. 'Charlotte, do you fancy having a quick ride with Hamish?'

And if it had been last week, Hamish *knew* the answer she'd have come up with, could almost hear her peal of laughter as she offered a saucy reply. But maybe the weekend had had more of an effect on her than he'd given her credit for, because all Charlotte did was give a weary nod. 'Where to?'

'City Hospital. I'm arranging the transport now—

do you want to tell his parents and then start getting him ready?'

'Sure.' Charlotte nodded. 'I'll just nip to the loo first.'

'I'll talk to the parents.' Hamish raked a hand through his hair and blew out a breath, and for the first time since Sunday his eyes met Charlotte's. Knowing what he was thinking, she shook her head.

'I think his mum's too upset to come with us—but it's your call.'

'I'll tell them to make their own way,' Hamish agreed. 'If they leave now, they might even beat us there.'

The helicopter ride there wasn't in the least uncomfortable. Hamish was so focused on Jordan, Charlotte could have been naked beside him and he'd hardly have noticed. But by the time they'd handed him over to the experienced team on ICU, by the time they'd been informed that the helicopter crew were heading back to base for refuelling and a staff changeover, the thought of two hours stuck in the back of an ambulance with Charlotte was the last thing on Hamish's wish list.

Charlotte's, too, it would seem.

Sitting back on the empty stretcher, she didn't even attempt conversation, just stared out the tinted windows with a drink bottle pressed to her face as Hamish considered asking the driver to speed things along and turn on the sirens.

'Seems a shame to waste it.' Smiling, but with her heart clearly not in it, looking and sounding nothing like the old Charlotte, she gestured to the empty stretcher, but Hamish soon realized that for once she wasn't making a joke.

'You don't mind if I lie down?'

He didn't bother answering and Charlotte didn't bother waiting, just clipped herself onto the stretcher and pulled the blanket around her, closing her eyes and proceeding to sleep all the way to Camberfield as Hamish finally got the message.

He didn't need to worry about avoiding her.

He'd already lost her.

CHAPTER NINE

'NICE night?' Trying for polite and holding a fretfully dozing Bailey, Hamish barely looked up as she clipped in wearing high heels and yet another very sexy skirt. Her face flushed, eyes glittering Charlotte jumped at the sound of Hamish's voice, then, realising he was nursing Bailey, tiptoed to the sink so as not to wake him.

'It was okay, I guess!' Too parched to even get a glass, Charlotte held her hair back and gulped from the running tap. 'Dancing's thirsty work.'

'It must be,' Hamish said, as she rummaged through the cupboard and, locating a large glass, filled it up. 'There's some headache tablets in the cupboard,' he added with a dry edge, 'just in case you need them in the morning.'

'I haven't got a hangover.' She actually sounded irritated. 'I haven't even had a drink.' Collapsing on the sofa, she gave a low laugh. 'I'm just exhausted, I guess.'

'Tell me about it…'

They sat in *almost* amicable silence for about five seconds.

'You know I won't be around Thursday or Friday—I'm going to clear out Mum's. So if you're on call…'

'We'll manage fine,' Hamish interrupted, and whether or not they would, he knew now that it wasn't really her concern.

'God, there's just so much to do,' Charlotte moaned. 'I've decided that that must be why I'm so tired—I'm exhausted in advance, thinking of all I have to do.'

Was she really expecting him to offer to come and help? He couldn't be positive, but he was sure she was fishing—even though yawning her head off and bemoaning her lot was a tactic he hadn't seen her use yet!

'Well, it's lucky, then, that you've got Trevor and his wife helping.'

'I guess,' Charlotte said, and then cheered up a touch. 'They're brilliant—in fact, by the time I get up there it will probably be half done. I'll have the place blitzed and locked up!'

'And you'll be done!' Hamish gave a tight smile.

'Finally!' Charlotte yawned then got up, filled her glass again and bade him goodnight, only remembering to tiptoe as far as the hallway, then clattering up the noisily up the stairs and waking up Bailey.

She didn't seem to care about *anything*, Hamish thought savagely as a now thoroughly awake Bailey jumped off his knee and, seizing the moment, delighted at his sudden freedom, wandered around the room.

Pack up the family home and hand over the keys—done!

Squeeze out a quick tear for an old nag—then get over it.

Shag Hamish on Sunday—why not?

Then go out dressed to the nines with Cameron on Tuesday—sure!

'Don't touch!' Hamish snapped to attention as Bailey's two-year-old hands, like mini-radars, instantly located the forbidden fruits in the lounge room—only instead of the television remote it was one of Charlotte's boxes he was familiarising himself with.

'Give that to me!' Hamish said in a loud whisper, attempting to wrestle a fistful of photos from Bailey's tight grip without crumpling them up altogether, making a mental note to apologise in the morning and get them repaired if that were possible, but all mental notes were discarded as he stared down at the picture in his hand: a pretty little girl, maybe seven or eight years old, was smiling widely back at him, her eyes staring directly into the camera as she offered a wide, beautiful smile without even a hint of a crooked tooth, her perfect ears framing a perfect face.

Strange that such a pretty picture could stir up such anger, but it did.

She was really that manipulative—a minx just like her mother, Hamish thought, recalling how convincingly Charlotte had won over little Andy, recalling how easily she'd stared into his little face and had said exactly what he had needed to hear in an attempt to win him over…

How she'd reeled Trevor in—insisting she'd manage yet getting his help all the same…

What was that line she'd fed the vet about Scottie being a disabled kids' pony to get out of paying the bill?

The line she'd fed *him* too about being broke, stopping him in his tracks just as he was about to send her away.

What an idiot! Raking his hand through his hair, Hamish actually felt sick, barely able to keep the disgust from his face as she came down again and refilled her glass.

'There's a tap in the bathroom!' Hamish said nastily. 'In case you haven't noticed, I am trying to get him to sleep.'

'Sorry!' Vague and distracted, she barely looked up as she headed for the cupboard. 'Maybe I will have a headache tablet after all—I think I must be coming down with something.'

'Help yourself!' Hamish said, sitting grim-faced on the sofa as she headed back upstairs. He promised himself that she'd never look after Bailey again—that when she came back from her trip on Friday he'd give her the weekend to find somewhere else. 'Help yourself,' Hamish said again as he heard her close the door of her bedroom. 'You usually do!'

'Come on now, Charlotte, snap to it!' Helen barked. 'You know, I would like to get to my bed sometime before lunchtime.'

'Sorry!' Shaking her head as if to clear it, Charlotte re-counted the ampoules of morphine and verified the number—the normally rapid task of checking the drugs at handover was taking for ever this morning, and Hamish rolled his eyes as he sat at the nurses' station, trying to get a basic patient history out of a *very* untogether Cameron.

'Did you bother to speak the patient at all?' Hamish snapped. 'Or are you just going by what was written on her referral letter?'

'She's got expressive dysphasia,' Cameron said for the third time. 'I can't make out what it is she's trying to tell me.'

'I'll try.' Helen came over and attempted to soothe troubled waters—expressive dysphasia was frustrating for the patient and the staff, the patient having an inability to say the words that they were trying to, confusion layering on exasperation at the recipient's inability to understand. 'I've been in with her, Hamish, and she really is difficult to make head nor tail of, the poor lamb.'

'But you're supposed to be going off duty,' Hamish pointed out. 'You shouldn't have to stay behind just because my resident can't get his act together.'

'Young Cameron stayed behind for me last night.' Helen was used to dealing with fractious doctors and was more than a match for Hamish. 'In fact, he should have been off duty at six, but ended up staying here till well past midnight—so, instead of scolding him for us all to hear, why don't you send him to the canteen for some breakfast and a couple of shots of coffee?'

'You were here last night?' Hamish's eyes jerked to Charlotte, then away. What the hell did it matter who she had been with last night? It was no longer his concern. 'Why didn't you say? Because I didn't give you a chance...' Hamish answered his own question with a sigh. 'What was the problem?'

'Nothing. I was waiting for the orthos to come down

and reduce a dislocated shoulder. I wanted to watch and the place got busy and I ended up getting caught up…you know how it is.'

Hamish didn't get a chance to either answer or apologise. The phone trilled loudly and from her grim expression as she dropped the receiver into the cradle and ran for Resus Hamish knew that this conversation would have to resume later.

'Paediatric arrest!' Helen was snapping red dots onto the cardiac monitor as she spoke. 'A two-year-old boy. He'll be here any second—they only live a few minutes away so the paramedics did a scoop and run….'

And seeing Hamish's face, Charlotte knew what must be flashing through his mind, saw him let out a breath as his brain must surely remind him that Bailey was safely in crèche. But Hamish wasn't about to relax. The two-year-old on his way in was someone else's son who was clearly in dire straits. A scoop and run was literally that—the paramedics making the decision that, rather than initiating treatment at the scene, hospital was urgently needed. Sirens were already screaming outside, blue lights flashing as Charlotte raced to the ambulance bay and opened the ambulance door before it had even halted. The paramedic threw down the paediatric-sized ambubag and jumped out with his little mottled bundle, one hand working the tiny chest as, still running fast but with an increasingly heavy heart, Charlotte followed him into Resus, knowing, knowing, knowing from that one tiny glimpse and the paramedic's face they were already way too late.

* * *

'He's gone…' Hamish stared at the monitor and then flicked his torch into the babe's eyes as Charlotte resumed compressions, the anaesthetist racing in and taking over the airway, but Hamish shook his head.

'But he's still warm!' Charlotte urged, knowing he was right but wanting so badly for him to be wrong.

'He is,' the breathless paramedic agreed, because it was a vital detail—the temperature of the boy was a good indication as to how long he had been down, and despite his appalling appearance this little one was *still* warm.

Still warm! Charlotte wanted to scream, but she didn't, just kept pushing on his chest until Hamish put out a hand to stop her.

'He was febrile,' Hamish said grimly. 'That's why he feels warm—but he's been dead a little while.'

'Poor pet!' Four decades into emergency nursing, Helen's voice was thick with emotion as Hamish, his face set but his hands supremely gentle, examined him, turning the little body over looking for a rash, looking for any signs of the thief that had come in and robbed this little boy of his life. 'He might have had a convulsion with the fever, there's vomit in his airway. Did you give him mouth to mouth?'

The paramedic nodded. 'On the way from the ambulance to here.'

'Then we'd better cover you with antibiotics. Don't go just yet. Where are the parents?'

'On their way. He's a twin, they're just getting the neighbour in to look after the other one.'

'He's a twin?' Charlotte's voice was aghast.

'Identical...' the paramedic started, but the receptionist came over then, averting her eyes from the bed, trying to talk in her normal efficient voice and no doubt just wanting to run.

'The parents just arrived.'

'If he's a twin then the other one needs to be seen and admitted,' Charlotte interrupted, but Hamish didn't need to be told, he just carried on talking in a calm voice to the receptionist.

'I'll come and speak to them now. Could you take them into the interview room? And could you also ring the switchboard for me? Tell them to hold off paging me till further notice unless it's extremely urgent.'

'We need to get the other one in...' Charlotte's voice was rising with each word and Hamish frowned at her to be quiet. 'We need the other little boy—were they sharing a cot?'

'I'm going to talk to the parents.'

'Hamish!' She grabbed his shirtsleeve as he went to walk out. 'You have to get the other one in. He could have—'

'I do know what I'm doing, thank you, Charlotte!' Hamish barked, angry not at her now but at the vile job that lay ahead. 'First I have to tell the parents their son's dead and *then* I tell them that their other child may be at risk. Now, will you, please, let go of my arm so that I can get on with this bastard of a job?'

'It's okay, pet!' Exhausted, Helen was frowning in concern as Charlotte gulped down a glass of water in the staffroom kitchen, her hand shaking so much she was spilling most of it. 'It gets to us all. I've been doing this job forty years but I can picture every little face—'

'I'm going home.' Charlotte interrupted her attempts at comfort. 'I don't feel very well.'

'You're upset. Don't go dashing off. You need to stay and—'

'It's not about the baby.' Charlotte shook her head firmly. 'I didn't feel well when I came on duty—I think I must be coming down with something. I've got a couple of days off coming up.'

'Charlotte, you know we're short of staff this morning. Can you at least stay till we can arrange some cover?'

'Sorry…' Brushing past her boss, Charlotte didn't even offer an excuse. 'I really can't, Helen. I'm going home.'

'Shouldn't you be in bed?' His face was grey but Hamish offered his colleague a sympathetic smile.

'Oh, I won't be going there for while.' Helen touched his arm, differences long forgotten, concern etched on her kind face. 'Are you okay, Hamish? That must have been awful for you, especially with little Bailey being the same age.'

'Not really,' he admitted, then sighed.

'How were the parents?' Helen started, but she already knew the answer, nodding as Hamish shook his head and declined to answer that question yet, just offering the usual one.

'Why do we do it, Helen?'

'I've no idea,' Helen answered . 'I ask myself the same question every blessed day.'

'I guess we all do…' Peering down at his pager, which was bleeping, Hamish gave a sigh and turned it off.

'Do you want me to bring you a drink to the nurses' station? I've got an instant soup in my bag.'

'What flavour?'

'One of those fancy ones—with croutons and noodles and everything. I'll even shake in a pepper sachet for you.'

'Sounds great.' Hamish gave a wan smile. 'Oh, and I was just on my way to find Charlotte—she seemed a bit upset. Could you tell her that the other twin's being bought in now? The paramedics have gone to get him.'

'She's gone.'

'Gone?'

'Yep.' Shrewd eyes stared back at Hamish. 'She says that she doesn't feel well. I have to be honest here—I don't know if she was telling the truth.'

'Well, she was out partying last night…'

'She was having one of her salsa dancing lessons,' Helen corrected him.

Hamish frowned. 'Salsa? Charlotte's taking salsa lessons?'

'Haven't you seen the noticeboard? Every Tuesday at the community centre, then they hold a dance there on a Friday or Saturday to strut their stuff. She's re-cruited half the unit…' Helen's voice was suddenly serious. 'I'm worried about her, Hamish.'

'About Charlotte?' He gave a slightly incredulous

laugh. 'Oh, I wouldn't worry too much about her, Helen, or she'll end up sleeping in your spare room.'

'Meaning?'

'Nothing,' Hamish sighed, angry with himself for being taken in but disappointed that he'd let some of it out. Whatever he privately thought of her, he had no right to bring her private life to work. No right at all. Charlotte was hardly the first or last to take a sick day when she didn't need it and Hamish did his best on her behalf to make up for his indiscretion.

'Now that I think of it, she was a bit peaky-looking this morning,' he offered rather unconvincingly, 'Maybe she's coming down with something—'

'I'm not worried that she's sick, Hamish.' Helen interrupted. 'This morning really upset her.'

'A two-year-old just died, Helen. *Everyone's* upset.'

'Yes—but we're not all running out the door. In fact, when I've sorted out some cover and grabbed a few hours' sleep, I might head over and see her. You don't mind if I go to your home?'

'Feel free.' Hamish shrugged and Helen went to bustle off but then changed her mind.

'You know, she never moans, you never hear that girl moaning about a single thing, which is great, of course, but it got me thinking.' Worried eyes met Hamish's and all of a sudden he was worried, too, all the little questions he had asked himself joining up into one big one. 'Is anyone really *that* happy with their lot in life?'

Hamish wasn't known for hiding in his office, yet, if the department had allowed it, he would have.

Thoughts about Charlotte blew in like a blizzard all through the day, but they never got a chance to settle—his time consumed with grief-stricken relatives on top of his usual workload and a staff that was, thanks to Charlotte's rapid departure and the failure to find a replacement, struggling to keep up with the load. But by two o'clock he couldn't stand it any longer. He handed over his pager to his registrar and for the first time in memory took a lunch-break at home, his stomach gnawing not with hunger but with something he couldn't identify—scolding himself the whole drive home for being unable just to blitz her from his mind.

'Seems you were right!' Helen gave a tight smile as he pulled up in the driveway. 'She's gone out for the day.'

'She could be at the doctor's.'

'For five hours?' Helen's eyebrows shot up to her hairline. 'I stopped by on my way home this morning. I think I'll stop worrying about Charlotte and get some well-earned rest—I'm back in that godforsaken place tonight. I really believed that little minx when she told me that she was going home.'

He barely even said goodbye to Helen, just let himself into the house, appalled at how empty it felt, even with her fat cat running up the hallway and her happy spaniel following suit to jump up to greet him.

For once he didn't notice or care as the pair, sensing weakness, followed him up the stairs. Pushing open her bedroom door, seeing the neatly made bed, inhaling her delicious scent, he then closed the door and went downstairs. The cups, the plates were all as they'd been this morning and a sense of foreboding filling him as he realised she hadn't been…

Home.

Yes, she was, he realized. She was at her mum's.

Relaxing a touch, Hamish filled the kettle. She'd just headed up there early, that was all.

Making a sandwich, he settled on the couch for his lunch, but still he couldn't switch off. He took one bite of it then put it down—that horrible knot in his stomach gnawing away at him as his eyes came to rest on her pile of boxes.

It was the least noble thing he'd ever done—a complete invasion of privacy, Hamish told himself. Only he wasn't listening. Instead, he was opening a lid and feeling sick to the stomach, somehow sensing before he even saw it what he was about to find.

There she was… He held the picture in his hand for a second and stared at the pretty, familiar face, turning it over and reading the handwriting on the back, before reaching in and pulling out a few more photos, screwing his eyes closed when his shuffling pulled up an ace, his eyes closing in regret for a second before opening again.

And there was Charlotte.

His heart contracted with love at the angry, pinched face that glared in the vague direction of the camera, at a little girl who was sure she wasn't beautiful *hating* having her photo taken. Working his way through, peering at her life, each photo lacerated him further, if that were possible, he could see her struggling to keep up with the sister that looked so much like her, but who had developed so much earlier into a beauty, watching her trying so hard to fit in. There she was again, hugging a much younger Scottie, actually smiling this time—utterly unaware that her photo was being taken.

'Poor Charlotte.' His voice halted, his heart stilling as he realised all she must have been through that morning, hearing again the urgency in her voice as she'd begged him to get in the other twin.

When she'd spoken to Andy she'd been telling the truth.

'Bastards!'

He said it again, sneered it at the unknowns who had made this little girl's life hell—but it was more directed at himself.

He'd shrugged her off, snapped at her when she'd begged him to bring in the other twin, had accused her, in his own mind, of not caring, not understanding. Only now did he realise that she'd understood more than most. And if the past few days had been awkward, for the first time he truly regretted their one night of love. Wished for different reasons that he'd held her just a little bit longer before kissing her, wished he'd spent just a bit more time trying to get inside that beautiful complicated mind.

'Why didn't you tell me?' Hamish moaned to the photo as the phone trilled beside him.

'Work said you were home…' It was Belinda, checking up on him. 'I haven't heard from you for a few days—I just wanted to check that things were okay.'

'Things are fine,' Hamish answered, staring at a picture of Charlotte and her sister. 'I just wanted an hour away from the place.'

'Yeah, I don't blame you.' Belinda gave a sympathetic sigh. 'I heard about the two-year-old when I was doing clinic this morning—it must have been awful.'

'He was a twin.'

'Poor little thing, just taken like that…' Belinda answered, and for the first time, and completely without malice, she said entirely the wrong thing, Hamish's hand gripping the phone as she forgot about the person who would possibly miss that little boy most. 'And those poor, poor parents…makes you wonder how they'll cope. Hey, Hamish…' He closed his eyes as she changed the subject. 'I'm thinking of starting those salsa lessons Charlotte's organised.'

'You?'

'Yep, me.' Belinda laughed. 'Rick's delighted—he wasn't at first, but when I showed him the new outfit I'd bought and Charlotte says that I have to get shoes…'

How *did* she cope?

Hanging up the phone, Hamish pondered the question that had so riled him when others had asked him.

Only he actually tried to answer it.

She coped by smiling…by keeping on going when her horse died or her mother upped and moved interstate. She coped by pushing her feelings right down.

Charlotte coped because she had to, because she had no choice, he told himself. She coped however she could—just as he had in the past eighteen months, and if she wasn't ready for a relationship then that was her right…

If she didn't want to take on him and his son, Hamish

could more than understand. God, he was a miserable bastard, Hamish thought with a dry smile. Most guys would kill to have her doing a salsa step and shimmying in front of them—any man worth his salt would kill for a night of no-strings sex with a woman like Charlotte. Try taking *that* tale of woe down the pub and expect an ounce of sympathy—they'd laugh him all the way out of there!

He'd say sorry, Hamish decided, just bite the bloody bullet and tell her that he'd found out about her twin, tell her…

Charlotte's mewing cat broke his introspection and Hamish got up to feed her—or him, he could never quite remember—but food wasn't on Maisy's mind. Instead, he rubbed his massive body against Hamish's legs and miaowed more loudly as Hamish glanced at his watch.

'Was that the problem?' Hamish asked as he filled his water bowl and plonked it down, watching as Maisy lapped furiously. 'She's got a cheek, forgetting to give you water considering how much she guzzles…' he started, but didn't finish. Seeing her lying exhausted out on the stretcher yesterday, standing in the kitchen last night, popping out headache tablets, her flushed face as she'd gulped water from the tap, hearing her footsteps as she'd clattered up the stairs to get to the loo all through the night, the utter weariness in her voice as she'd contemplated the massive task that lay ahead over the next couple of days.

She wasn't just upset—Charlotte *was* ill.

Only she didn't know.

Reaching for his car keys, punching numbers into his mobile, he called his sister and then the hospital, told them something urgent had come up and that for now they'd just have to cope without him…because something urgent had come up. Calling real-estate agent after real-estate agent as he ignored the speed limit, it took his most authoritative doctor's voice and eventually a shouting match to extricate the address of a house on acreage, owned by a Ms Josie Porter, that settled on Monday and praying that he could get to Charlotte soon.

He'd thought the very worst of her.

And all the time she'd been doing her very best.

CHAPTER TEN

'HANG in there, young lady!'

Seeing her lying on the bathroom floor, and gently rolling her on her side, Hamish popped on a mask and turned on the portable cylinder of oxygen he'd brought. Even though he had to call for help, even though his arm was bleeding from breaking a window to get in, Hamish dealt with the necessities first.

He'd diagnosed her diabetes at the house, could smell the ketones her body was producing on her breath, didn't really need to do a blood sugar to confirm his diagnosis. But he followed procedure, an IV line already in and hanging from the shower, insulin already drawn up, before the reading came through, then delivering her the first of the drugs she so desperately needed, before punching in the emergency number and summoning assistance. Then he quickly strapped up his arm, watching her all the time and wondering, with limited supplies, what more he could do.

What would Charlotte want him to do?

Seeing this funny, proud independent woman lying

on the floor, where she had clearly been for hours, it wasn't that hard a question to answer.

He'd better cope with the *real* necessities!

Racing through the house, he located her bedroom, knowing it was hers in an instant, not from the photos on the wall or the bags in the door but from two twin beds in the room, imaging the agony she would have silently endured, watching the charity shop take them the following morning.

Opening her little overnight bag, Hamish pulled out some fresh knickers and leggings and paused for a second at the door...

Maybe she had been fishing for him to come and help her, Hamish thought. Maybe in her own round-about way, she had, for once, been asking for help.

'This isn't how it looks,' Hamish muttered to himself, wrestling off her damp jeans and dressing her in clean knickers and leggings, and doing a quick tidy-up of the floor, relief flooding him when finally the sound of sirens could be heard.

The sound of boots crashed through the door and raced up the stairs and Hamish called out to them. Nameless paramedics changing over oxygen cylinders and attaching her to monitors as Hamish told them all he knew.

'What's the story?'

'Newly diagnosed diabetic.' Hamish gulped. 'Hyper-glycaemic coma—she has ketoacidos. I took a blood glucose. I think she's been lying here for hours.'

'When did you find her?'

'Twenty minutes ago.'

'You're sure about that?' The paramedic frowned, and rightly so. A patient this sick, one who had been lying there so long, should surely appear a little less dignified!

'I cleaned up a bit.' Hamish, met the paramedic's eyes. 'I'm a consultant at Camberfield, I mean Northern District Emergency. Believe me, she really is as bad as she seems...' Staring down at Charlotte, he didn't notice the paramedic's eyes widen in recognition.

'Sorry, Doc. I didn't realise it was you.'

'Just worry about her,' Hamish urged, stepping back a bit as they set to work, feeling completely useless as he stood in the hall and they negotiated the stretcher out of the bathroom.

'Just move back a bit, Doc, would you?'

Which he did. He stood at the door of her bedroom and stared at the two single beds that had been and surely always would be her world, swearing that if he lived to a hundred then that was what he would do...worry about Charlotte and make sure that she was happy.

'I should have called an ambulance the second I guessed.'

'And told them to break into her mother's home on a hunch...' Helen was screwing in yet another IVAC around Charlotte's bed. Adding yet another drug to yet another intravenous line as Charlotte lay there, still unconscious, lips raw and cracked, her face dry and flushed under the oxygen mask, her body wrapped in a space blanket to conserve her temperature as they struggled to get her blood sugar down and balance her dangerously abnormal electrolyte and bicarbonate levels.

'A bit more than a hunch. I'm an emergency consultant—she's been guzzling water and running to the loo every five minutes, it should have been obvious she had diabetes. I thought she was flushed because she'd been out s—' He snapped his mouth closed, hating how cheap he'd thought her.

'Doing her blessed salsa dancing!' Helen laughed. 'She's as mad as anything—do you know, she begged me to come along with her? Said it would fun. I'm sixty years old and she was telling me to dress like a tart—put on high heels and a sexy skirt…'

'That's Charlotte! She doesn't know when to give in…' Hamish laughed but it changed in the middle and he had to actually grit his teeth together to stop himself breaking down.

'It was actually a lot of fun!' Helen corrected as Hamish wilted—that wild group of friends and lovers he'd envisaged so, so pathetically wrong. 'She's hardly been here five minutes and she's got a whole group of us going out dancing—even Mike the old porter comes along when he can. Did you not read the notice she put up, inviting us all along? I never thought I'd go, let alone have such a laugh, but heaven knows we could all use one, working in this place. I told her I'll be back at it next week when I finish nights! Hey, Charlotte…' she spoke into her ear, 'we might have to give it a miss next week—but as soon as you've got all your regime sorted, we're going out dancing again!

'Come on, now,' Helen said to Hamish as his face started to crumple. She summoned another nurse to Charlotte's gurney. 'We're going for a coffee, and don't even think of arguing.'

He didn't.

Since he'd found her on the floor, he hadn't left her side, willing the paramedics to hurry, cursing the fact the local hospital had closed down and working on her in the helicopter as she had been airlifted to his hospital. And not once had she opened her eyes, not once had she given any sign that she could hear him.

But this time round he knew that maybe she could.

This time he *knew* that there was hope, that with the right treatment, which she was getting, *this* woman he loved was going to be okay.

'Now, forgive me for being nosy…' Helen handed him a steaming mug as she gave herself permission to boldly cross the line. 'I'm assuming there's a bit of romance in the air between the two of you.'

'Leave it, Helen.'

'I will not,' Helen chided. 'Did you break up? Is that why you thought she was out with another young man?'

'We didn't break up because we were never together,' Hamish muttered.

'Well, excuse me for getting it wrong.' Helen patted his knee. 'But lately I've never seen you looking better—well, not since Emma was here anyway. And more relaxed,' she added, 'and chatting about young Bailey doing so well, like any proud father.'

'I've always been a proud father.'

'You just didn't have a moment to notice!' She stood up to go. 'Till Charlotte arrived, that is!'

'We were sort of…' Hamish's voice halted her in the door. 'Well, one night… Oh, just leave it.' He gave a shrug of irritation. 'You wouldn't understand.'

'Of course I wouldn't—you think I've never had sex! Five kids and I've no idea how they got here—and forty years working in Emergency and hearing tales that would make your hair curl, yet I still believe that everyone's a virgin on their wedding night. So don't even try telling me, Hamish! Don't even try talking about it or asking someone you trust for a bit of help!'

'Close the door,' he groaned, embarrassed and appalled and scarcely able to believe he was about to discuss his rather sparse sex life with Helen, of all people. But what the hell, Hamish decided. She was a woman, wasn't she? And right now he needed all the help he could get in dealing with the most complicated one of them all!

'On Sunday her horse—I mean, her pony—had to be put down.'

'Poor pet—she must have been beside herself.'

'She didn't seem it.' Hamish shook his head. 'She was just, well, Charlotte. And then there was the house fire and then she *did* seem upset and the next thing…'

'I get the picture.'

'She dumped me the next morning.' He gave a dry, mirthless laugh. 'Greeted me with that happy smile and basically told me she had been having a rough night and I had been a better option than a sleeping tablet.' As

Helen gave a dubious frown, Hamish relented a touch. 'Well, not in so many words.'

'But that was how you took it?'

'Believe me, the message was pretty clear!'

'Did you not stop to think that maybe she was just getting in first?' When Hamish frowned, Helen elaborated. 'Before *you* dumped her.'

'Why would I dump her?' Hamish shook his head.

'Guilt over Emma. I mean, it's only been eighteen months…'

'As if I don't know that,' Hamish answered. 'You know, I never in my lifetime expected to feel this way again. Okay, maybe I did feel a bit guilty, but to tell you the truth I haven't had time to really think about it—I haven't stopped for breath since Charlotte came into my life. Why would I dump her when I'm crazy about her? Why would I get rid of the best thing that's happened to me in ages?'

'You told her all this, I assume?'

'She didn't give me a chance!' Hamish barked, and then softened. Helen was, after all, only trying to help. 'Charlotte's…complicated,' he attempted, but how could he tell Helen what he'd found out when he wasn't even supposed to know himself? How could he explain what he didn't yet understand?

'Did you ever ask her out for a good old-fashioned date?'

'Sort of. I tried a couple of times—asked her if she wanted to share a take-away on Friday…' Hamish attempted, realising as he said it how vague he had been. 'You've no idea how hard that was to do, Helen.'

'She was out dancing on Friday—you should have come along.'

'I thought she was out partying with hundreds of other men at a rave!' Hamish groaned.

'Oh, it was a rave!' Helen winked. 'Best Friday night out I've had in ages. I'm surprised she didn't ask you.'

'She did.' Hamish swallowed. 'Well, sort of.'

'Did you ever stop to wonder how hard that would have been for her? The notice has been up for a while now and you haven't shown a shred of interest in coming along.'

'I didn't even read it,' Hamish said glumly.

'There's a good case for virgins on their wedding nights!' Sounding far more like the old Helen, she stood up. 'Sex is the easy bit, Hamish, feelings are the ones that take a bit of working. But you lot…' Banding anyone under forty, and especially Hamish, with the hormones of an adolescent she wagged a finger at him. 'Well, you just jump on in without even bothering to talk. I suggest you give it a try.'

And he would, but not yet.

For now he sat through the night in Intensive Care. The receptionist had finally located her next of kin and he rang her mother, angry with Josie and disappointed for Charlotte that Josie took his reassuring words rather too literally, that by the end of the conversation Josie had, instead of trying to book a flight from Queensland and heading for the airport, decided to 'wait' and see how things looked in the morning.

And later, when things were looking up, when Charlotte, still groggy, had definitely turned the corner—he headed to Belinda's to say sorry for dumping his little boy on her again and to have a quick, longed-for cuddle with Bailey, glad, so glad and so very, very lucky to have a family that actually cared—a sister who a couple of weeks into a new job would ring in sick and look after her nephew, without asking for information, just accepting that her brother needed her to. Heading for home, he rang Trevor to check if everything was in order at the house and what, from this end, he could do. Then he fed the pets and walked the dog then packed her a little bag. Heading back to the hospital, he managed a wry smile as halfway out of the drive he turned back and added lipstick and her perfume to the toiletries—utter essentials where Charlotte was concerned.

Waiting, waiting for their time to talk.

Wondering what, if anything, Charlotte would have to say.

CHAPTER ELEVEN

'WON'T be a sec.' Charlotte smiled briefly up at him as he walked in—and he watched as she insisted to the nurse that she do her own blood sugar, pricking her finger without even a wince. 'Seven,' Charlotte dictated, boldly checking her drug chart for the sliding scale of insulin she had been written up for until her blood sugar stabilised. 'So no need for anything for now.'

Hamish could only roll his eyes at her audacity.

Six hours out of Intensive Care and she was sitting up in bed in *that* nightdress, wearing lipstick and running the show.

'You're looking better.'

'I feel it!' Charlotte nodded. 'I'm going to start giving myself insulin tomorrow!' She even made it sound exciting. 'Thanks so much for coming to get me…' As he sat on the bed beside her, Charlotte swallowed hard and took his hand. 'I didn't say that very well.' Staring up at him, she took a deep breath. 'Thank you for saving my life—I'm very glad that you did.'

'I'm very glad that I did, too,' Hamish said, and he meant it—and not because he was a doctor and life was precious, not even because he loved her, but because the world was nicer place with people like Charlotte in it. And even if what they had shared could never be sustained, even if it had only been transitory, *his* world was a better place because of it.

'I should have worked it out myself,' she said. 'I was in the loo every five minutes, drinking gallons, and I felt *awful*. I just thought I had flu or something. It was all so quick. I guess I was upset, what with…' Her voice trailed off but Hamish wasn't going to let her leave it there.

'With?'

'Scottie and everything.'

'The house fire…' Hamish prompted, and she nodded.

'Us?' He was scared to look at her, but he did so, holding his breath until finally, hesitantly she nodded.

'I guess.'

And as relieved as he was that she nodded, it was Hamish who hesitated before going on.

'The little twin boys coming in must have been hell for you.'

He watched her still dry tongue bob out, watched as she dragged it over lips that, despite several layers of lip-gloss, were still chapped and sore, before carefully selecting her words. 'It was awful for everyone.'

'But hell for you.' Tears actually sparkled in her eyes, but she blinked them back. 'I know about Cassie.' When she didn't say anything, just held onto his hands, Hamish spoke on. 'Well, I don't know about her, but I found this.' He pulled a picture out of his pocket and placed it on her lap, watched as she closed her eyes rather than look at it. 'Bailey got into your boxes…' Hamish started then checked himself. Lies had no place here. 'That's not true. I actually found a picture of Cassie the other night. I thought…'

'That I'd lied to Andy.'

'I thought that you'd lied about a lot of things— only you don't lie, do you?'

She shook her head then changed her mind and stared at him. 'Just once.'

'When you weren't at home, I knew something was wrong, I just couldn't work out what. I know I should-n't have gone through your private things…'

'You were snooping?'

'Yes,' Hamish shamefacedly admitted, confused when she smiled.

'That's okay. I snoop all the time. Can't help my-self!'

'I thought she was you.'

'She is.' Finally Charlotte opened her eyes and picked up the photo—stared at two incredibly similar yet very different faces, her slender finger tracing her sister's. 'Or was. To tell you the truth, sometimes I don't know where Cassie starts and I finish.

'Does that sound mad?'

'Maybe to someone who never had a twin.'

'Where do we go when we die, Hamish?' Charlotte asked. And though he'd had his share of difficult ques-tions, this one took the cake. 'All that love, all that energy, all that passion…'

And suddenly he *did* know what she was talking

about, suddenly Charlotte was voicing the question he'd asked of himself long and late into the night.

And for the first time he could take a stab at answering it.

'I think it's shared around with the people who need it or the people that can help...' Hamish offered. 'I know that Bel and I never really got on—we were always arguing about something or nothing, and then Emma died and she was just there for me in a way I never could have imagined she would be...'

'It's like getting on a bus.' Charlotte lay back on the pillows and stared up at the ceiling. 'This bus called pain comes round the corner and you don't want to get on but, like it or not, you do and there's all these people helping you, all these people who have been there, done that... Like Helen. She lost her husband.'

'Helen and Eugene have been married for forty years...' Hamish shook his head. 'You've got that wrong, Charlotte, they've got five kids.'

'And the first one had a dad called Declan...' Charlotte gave a tired smile. 'She was sixteen and she loved him.'

'Helen?'

'Yep...' Her tired eyes tried to focus, but didn't manage it too well. 'She's been on the bus.'

'Go to sleep, Charlotte.'

'I want to talk.'

'We will.' Hamish said. 'Now go to sleep.'

She woke up to her sister's smiling face, propped up against the water jug, and she missed her more in that moment than she ever had, knew that she would miss her for ever.

'I sort of try and live for both of us.'

Hamish truly didn't know what to say to her, had been dozing in the chair beside her, and he wished he could understand how she felt, but understood he couldn't, so just told her the little he knew. 'I read that the death of a twin, especially an identical twin, is one of the most unique and hardest of griefs to bear.'

'I was *always* a twin.' She stared over to him as if willing him to understand. 'Till I was fifteen I was a twin, and so was Cassie—not a sister, but a twin—that was who *we* were.

'I was the ugly one, though.' How he wanted to interrupt her, but he didn't dare, knew that hearing what she had to say was the only way he could even *begin* to understand. 'I was a typical second twin, smaller, weaker—or that was how it seemed.

'I had a few "problems"—mild cerebral palsy, a lazy eye. There was actually quite a list, whereas Cassie, it seemed, had none. She was everything I aspired to be, everything I almost was.'

'Were you jealous?'

'No.' She frowned as if really thinking about it. 'No, I was just in awe. She was so gorgeous, just so confident and outgoing—everyone adored her. All my problems slowly got fixed—riding was great for my limp, I had braces, my ear was pinned back. Self-confidence takes a bit more hard work, though.'

'You still felt…'

'Ugly!' Charlotte said it for him. 'Yep, and I was still

picked on like crazy because I figured that was all I deserved. Cassie kept telling me to get over it—to just get out there and have fun but when I wasn't with her I was just such a shy, lonely little thing. I struggled through school, did my riding, my homework, and that was about it. Then we both got flu, right at the same time—it was always like that for us. If Cassie had toothache, I had it ten minutes later. If I got sent to sick bay with period pain, Cassie was already lying on the bed with a hot-water bottle. We shared a room and we were both just so sick and Mum was more worried about me, you know, what with me being a bit weaker and everything—only it turned out I wasn't the weak one, not where it mattered anyway. They found out on autopsy that she had a valve problem with her heart. It had never been picked up and the virus was just too much for her.'

'Oh, Charlotte.' It was Hamish's eyes that were filling with tears, Hamish feeling like breaking down, but finally he was beginning to glimpse why it wasn't Charlotte, *finally* he was beginning to understand a little of what made her *her*!

'They didn't tell me for ages. We were both taken to hospital—but we were put in separate rooms. I hated that. I hated not knowing what was happening. I thought all the concern was because of me whereas the doctors were trying to work out what the hell was wrong with her, sure I was going to collapse with it too at any moment. I didn't know she was dying in the next room and they were all too worried how I'd react to tell me.'

'You didn't get to say goodbye?'

'They didn't tell me till two days afterwards. Oh, I know they thought they were doing the right thing—when she died they still didn't know she had a congenital problem with her heart—and they were worried how the shock would affect me. But even so, you'd think they'd at least…' She gave a small sniff, her eyelashes heavy with tears that she wouldn't allow to fall. 'I should have been with her.'

'Yes.' Hamish nodded, because she should have.

'Even all these years on and with all I know, I wish I'd been allowed to take that risk.'

'I'm so, so sorry they did that,' Hamish said, and even if it couldn't possibly be his fault he was sorry on behalf of his profession—sorry for what they had made her miss.

'I'm not going to cry.' Blue eyes stared back at him completely devoid of tears now. 'If you're waiting for me to start sobbing…'

'I'm not.' Hamish shook his head as she grew more insistent.

'Because I did all that and it didn't work for me. I think I cried for a whole year solid after she died.'

'What did work for you, Charlotte?'

'Realising how lucky I was to be alive,' Charlotte answered without a beat of hesitation. 'Realising that the best thing I could do for Cassie was to live for both of us, to take all the confidence, all that energy she must have left somewhere and just enjoy this wonderful life—which I do.'

'And it shows.' He held her hand just a little bit harder, understood her a bit deeper and loved her a whole lot more. 'When you're better, when you're ready…' He paused with nervousness and again she dived in.

'You want me to leave? Hamish, I fully understand.'

'No, Charlotte, you don't. I want you to stay.' He couldn't believe that she still didn't get it. 'What I'm trying to say is that when you're better, if you want to, I'd love it if you'd come out with me for a drink or dinner—not just a curry at home because I haven't got a babysitter, not joining in on a boozy hospital social night, but—'

'You want me to come on a date with you?' Charlotte blinked.

'A real old-fashioned date.' He gave a wry smile. 'According to Helen, that's the way we're supposed to go about it.'

'So no torrid sex this time?'

'Not even a hint—that's for the married people apparently.'

'Oh!'

'Just a lot of talking and getting to know each other better…' Hamish said, appalled but laughing when she screwed up her nose.

'I preferred it our way!'

'Really?' Hamish frowned.

'Well, maybe a touch more talking,' she admitted, 'but we've just done that.'

'Charlotte.' He was still frowning. 'The kettle hadn't even boiled the next morning and you—'

'I thought you were going to ask me to leave.'

'Never!' Hamish said with certainty, but then it

wavered. 'I just don't know how you could ignore Bailey. It seemed as if you didn't want to know him.'

'Never!' Charlotte's voice was equally certain. 'I was sick and tired and terrified of breaking down if I so much as went near him…' She *was* nearly crying now. 'That was the one time I lied…' The honesty in her voice stilled him. 'It was never ever just "one of those things" to me.

'I love you, Hamish.' As easily as that she said it, and amazingly he accepted it.

'I know.'

'I know you must miss Emma…'

'I do.' Hamish nodded. 'I just never figured anyone could understand it, and I never figured on being happy again, and then you came along…and I think about ten seconds in I fell in love.'

'What took you so long?' Charlotte sniffed.

'You make my world brighter, just as you do with everyone you come in contact with, and I love your crazy perspective… But, Charlotte…' He pulled her into his arms, felt her tiny and fragile yet incredibly strong, and gave her one promise that she probably would never want repeated, but Hamish swore would last a lifetime. 'Every now and then…if it is all a bit much…you can lean on me for as long as it takes.'

'Then pick myself up and carry right on?'

'Absolutely,' he said softly. 'I'm here.'

So she did. She didn't cry, didn't do anything except let him hold her, let him stroke away the horror of the past few days, hold her as she got her mind around needles and blood sugars and ponies that died and mums that left, just let him hold her for as long as took to come right back up smiling.

'Better?' Hamish checked.

'Better.' Charlotte nodded, then changed her mind, resting her head back on his shoulder till she voiced what was worrying her now.

'I *really* liked the torrid sex.' She screwed her eyes closed as she said it and Hamish did the same, taking a deep breath as Charlotte held onto hers.

'Is that a proposal?'

'I think so.' Charlotte blinked into his chest. 'If Helen says that we *have* to wait till we're married, then I think it would be wrong to just…'

'I'll get a licence.'

'Please.' She pulled back and stared at him in exasperation. 'Well, go!'

'I think it takes a couple of weeks to organise.' Hamish grinned.

'Then you'd better hurry up,' Charlotte prompted. 'Maybe we should have our honeymoon before the wedding, lie on a beach somewhere fabulous with Bailey while I hurry up and get well.' She gave him a wink. 'Only we won't tell Helen. Well,' she demanded, 'what are you waiting for?'

'A kiss,' Hamish said, taking her chin in his hands and gently, tenderly kissing her sore chapped lips, torn between staying just a little bit longer or getting out there and planning their wonderful lives…

Either way it didn't matter.

EPILOGUE

HE WAS beyond surprises.

Just completely beyond them by now.

And walking into the family room after a very long day at work, he barely raised an eyebrow as the sat there at the sewing machine. It was supposed to be an antique, a decoration for the corner—he hadn't even known it worked, it was just this big, dusty, old black sewing machine that had come with the house, yet there she was, pushing layer upon layer of chiffon through and cursing like a sailor every time the needle buckled, and even though he could tell she'd been crying, Charlotte smiled as he came in.

'What time do you call this?'

'Way too late…' Hamish groaned. 'It got busy about ten minutes after your shift ended. Oh, and one of your many friends came—little Andy. He had a blood nose and broken tooth.'

'Oh, no…'

'Oh, yes.' Hamish grinned. 'He was goalie in soccer and the ball hit him in the face. He's doing great. His skin's a lot better and he's made a couple of friends.'

'Really?'

'Really.' Hamish smiled. 'How about you?'

'Well, I was okay…' She swallowed hard and Hamish waited for her to smile, only she didn't. Tears actually spilled out of those gorgeous eyes as she gestured towards Bailey, who was scribbling on a piece of paper and missing most of the edges, the coffee table covered in jagged red lines. 'He called me Dumb.'

'Dumb?' Hamish frowned, appalled and frankly stunned to see her like this. That a bit of cheek from Bailey could reduce her to tears had him completely baffled. 'Charlotte, he didn't mean it, he wouldn't even know what it means…it's just a word he's picked up in crèche…' Hamish started to laugh. 'Anyway, he can talk! Tell him he can't even spell his own name yet!'

'It's not that,' Charlotte gulped. 'He knows exactly what it meant! He said it about five times and he kept pointing to me—I think it's a cross between Charlotte and Mum!'

'Oh.' Hamish stood there as the news sank in.

'And then I got to thinking how you'd feel if he started calling me that—I mean, I know I'm not his real mum…'

'He adores you,' Hamish said softly. 'I adore you…' And for a tiny second he wasn't so strong. 'Emma would have adored you.'

'Promise?'

'Promise,' Hamish said as she leant against him, holding her as close as he could because on occasion she needed it and he wanted so much to say the right thing—to say she was the best thing that happened to

him and Bailey. But that would be cheating on Emma—
that would be cheating on another world, another life
that had been perfect as well. And for a moment it
wasn't Hamish holding Charlotte but the other way
around as he wondered how it was possible to love two
people, so very, very much.

'I'm out tomorrow night.' Charlotte broke into his
thoughts. 'Elsie's happy to drop in if you get called.'

'Fine.' He tried to smile, tried not to be irritated that
she'd missed how much this moment meant to him—
how strange it had felt to actually know that Bailey considered someone who wasn't Emma his mum.

Only he still hadn't quite worked Charlotte out.

Still couldn't quite grasp that she already had the
answers.

'Is it your salsa class?'

'Salsa?' Charlotte gave him an old-fashioned look.
'Why would I be sewing gold hoops onto chiffon for
salsa? I'm starting belly-dancing classes—I'm trying to
get a whole group of us to go. Didn't you see the notice
I put up at work?'

'Well, if Helen's going to that,' Hamish groaned, 'I'm
not even going to make up an excuse for not joining
you!'

'You won't have to.' Charlotte giggled. 'It's closed
doors—for women only. Apparently it's great for
strengthening you pelvic floor. Helen said—'

'Don't.' Hamish covered his ears. 'Don't even *start*
to tell me that she has stress incontinence—I have to
work with her tomorrow.'

'Helen said…' Charlotte smiled, pulling down his

hands and whispering into his ears in the way that had him wanting to give Bailey two-minute noodles and send him to bed very quickly. 'That belly dancing is great for the pelvic floor muscles…and especially good exercise for pregnant women.'

He hadn't expected that at all—every night it was a pleasure to come home, but tonight was the sweetest of them all.

'When did you find out?'

'Five minutes before my shift ended,' Charlotte said. 'I nicked a pregnancy testing kit from the cupboard. I'm sorry that I told Helen first—but you were stuck in Resus and I was sort of in a spin when I found out and I just needed to talk…'

And he could understand that, because Hamish felt like racing down the driveway and declaring to the world that they were having a baby. And just because he'd done this before it didn't diminish it, just because he'd been enthralled at the prospect of becoming a father it didn't mean it couldn't feel just as good again.

Charlotte Adams was carrying his baby, and on the very same day she'd become 'Dumb' to Bailey—that surely couldn't be put down to coincidence.

And there she was smiling because it was way better than crying, enjoying the good times rather than be-moaning her losses. But he could see her red-rimmed eyes so he held her all over again because he wanted to and, more importantly, because for a minute or two she needed it.

'It will be okay, won't it—what with my diabetes and everything?'

'It's going to be fine.' Hamish held her tighter. 'They'll just keep a closer eye on you and the baby…'

'I was going to look it up—you know, read about it…'

'Then you realised what a *dumb* thing that would be to do.' Hamish smiled into her hair. 'I'm pulling rank here and happily so—you're to let the doctors worry about dealing with your diabetes.'

'And you're going to let the obstetrician…' Charlotte responded.

'Touché!'

Still holding her, he ran an entranced hand over the soft mound of her stomach, still trying to fathom that this miracle was growing inside her.

'Funny how much you can love someone who isn't even here.' Gently for once, Charlotte broke into his thoughts and in her own sweet time and own very strange way she continued the conversation they'd been having a few minutes earlier. 'I mean it's just a few cells, a tiny little scrap that could be a he or a she or a them or an it—and yet I'm head over heels already, would move heaven and earth for someone who supposedly doesn't exist.'

'That's love, I guess,' Hamish said, his throat suddenly very tight. 'I never imagined loving another child as much as I love Bailey…'

'Oh, you will,' Charlotte said. 'I know that you will.'

And now so did Hamish.

'Just because Emma and Cassie aren't here any more, it doesn't mean their love has stopped,' Charlotte added gently, 'and it doesn't mean we can't keep right on loving them.' That she was so generous with her heart and that she could include Emma in this tender moment just blew him away. 'Anyway, enough of the sad stuff.' Wriggling out of his arms, she gave a quick sniff. 'You'd better sit down.'

'Why? Don't tell me you've got more news!'

'Don't be daft. Go on, go and sit down with Bailey.' Charlotte grinned, rummaging in her bag and putting on a quick flash of lipstick then picking up her mountains of chiffon as, with an almost weary sigh, Hamish joined Bailey and sat down, *knowing* what was coming and wondering if other couples did strange things like this. 'It's show time!'

Well, if they didn't, they should try it. Hamish grinned, watching as this most gorgeous haphazardly veiled woman danced and shimmied towards them, making them laugh when it would be easy to cry, taking an amazing moment and somehow making it just a little bit more so.

'Dumb!' Bailey cheered, squealing with delight and clapping to some imaginary rhythm, egging her on—as if she needed it—as Charlotte thrust her hips and gyrated towards them, looking nothing like a belly dancer but, hey, who cared about a minor detail like grace or rhythm when it was Charlotte who was dancing towards you?

Who needed anything else when they had love completely on their side?

THE ITALIAN COUNT'S BABY
by Amy Andrews

Nurse Katya Petrov believes her unborn baby needs its father. When the talented Italian surgeon Count Benedetto, with whom she spent one passionate night, finds out he is to be a daddy, he offers her marriage – *for the baby's sake*! Only Katya secretly longs for Ben to give her his heart.

THE NURSE HE'S BEEN WAITING FOR
by Meredith Webber

Beautiful nurse Grace O'Riordan has always been in love with sexy police officer Harry Blake. As a cyclone hits Crocodile Creek, Harry and Grace are forced together to save lives – jolting Harry into having emotions he never believed he'd feel again…

HIS LONG-AWAITED BRIDE
by Jessica Matthews

When his best friend, Marissa Benson, announces that she is engaged, unexpected longings are stirred up in Dr Justin St James. Furious that he's been so blind to the attraction between them for so long, Justin is determined to win Marissa as *his* wife!

FREE!

4 Books
and a surprise gift!

We would like to take this opportunity to thank you for reading this Mills & Boon® book by offering you the chance to take FOUR more specially selected titles from the Medical™ series absolutely FREE! We're also making this offer to introduce you to the benefits of the Mills & Boon® Reader Service™—

- ★ **FREE home delivery**
- ★ **FREE gifts and competitions**
- ★ **FREE monthly Newsletter**
- ★ **Exclusive Reader Service offers**
- ★ **Books available before they're in the shops**

Accepting these FREE books and gift places you under no obligation to buy, you may cancel at any time, even after receiving your free shipment. Simply complete your details below and return the entire page to the address below. You don't even need a stamp!

YES! Please send me 4 free Medical books and a surprise gift. I understand that unless you hear from me, I will receive 6 superb new titles every month for just £2.89 each, postage and packing free. I am under no obligation to purchase any books and may cancel my subscription at any time. The free books and gift will be mine to keep in any case.

M7ZEF

Ms/Mrs/Miss/Mr ....Initials ....
BLOCK CAPITALS PLEASE

Surname ....

Address ....

....

....Postcode ....

Send this whole page to:
UK: FREEPOST CN81, Croydon, CR9 3WZ

Offer valid in UK only and is not available to current Mills & Boon® Reader Service™ subscribers to this series. Overseas and Eire please write for details. We reserve the right to refuse an application and applicants must be aged 18 years or over. Only one application per household. Terms and prices subject to change without notice. Offer expires 30th November 2007. As a result of this application, you may receive offers from Harlequin Mills & Boon and other carefully selected companies. If you would prefer not to share in this opportunity please write to The Data Manager, PO Box 676, Richmond, TW9 1WU.

Mills & Boon® is a registered trademark owned by Harlequin Mills & Boon Limited.
Medical™ is being used as a trademark. The Mills & Boon® Reader Service™ is being used as a trademark.